Ab‹

An accountant by profession, wildlife conservationist and subscriber to various animal charities, lover of gardening, and growing exotic plants. Someone who has various pets, enjoys writing, loves various music, ancient history, cinema and the theatre, human cultures, traditions, religions and beliefs, a student of Lau Gar Kung Fu and interested in all other forms of the Martial Arts, helping to support cancer, arthritis, heart, and war veterans etc. Someone who is fascinated in evolution, green technologies, spiritual, and magic.

My view is to look after others as you would like to be looked after yourself, be a good custodian to all living things and the well-being of the planet.

Finally, if I can bring joy, excitement, and happiness to the readers, then I am truly content.

Best wishes

Chris Hayes-Brown

27/11/2021

Dedication

To those wonderful pets who I have had the honour to call my friends, it was a pleasure to have known them, my soul buddies, and companions in life, especially those that recently passed away. To Layla, Troy, Libby and Bramble, and those wonderful pets that have gone before. I miss you all so much, and God bless you.

To those wonderful people and organisations, the indigenous tribes who care for the animals, plants and habitats that we share with, thank you.

To all those animal lovers who have lost their wonderful pets, to their current pets, and the wonderful wildlife of our amazing world. 'Who we share this planet with', thank you, the world would not be the same without all of you.

To my family, to our beloved Honey and Ollie, my good friends, and amazing Facebook friends, work/business colleagues current and past, to the various societies that I am a member of.

But also I want to thank the publisher Austin Macauley and their fantastic staff from the bottom of my heart for making this dream come true.

Finally to those who have departed, the family members, friends and past work colleagues, that I have had the great pleasure of knowing, may you rest in eternal peace.

The opening theme tune – a dedication to Doris Troy – the song 'Just One Look'.

I dedicate these stories to those special animals that have played a part in my life: -

Especially to Layla who passed away on 24th September 2015 who we all miss very much, as for me, I will never forget her, it was an honour and privilege to have known her, she was a wonderful companion and friend. I will always love her, and with the tears in my eyes that I shred to this very day for my darling Layla and all the other amazing pets that are now in heaven.

To Ollie, Troy, Zulu, Sasha, Bam, Max, Sara, the German shepherds, to Honey and Heidi the Labradors, to Poppy, and Sasha the boxers, to Bruno the Rottweiler.

To Libby, Tao, Laura, Pickwick, Kim, Spectra, Sasha, and Lowyra the Siamese cats, to Kip, Tigger, Tabs, Fluff, Barnaby, Chi Chi the lovely domestic cats.

To Billy the cockatiel, to the silkie hens, the rabbits including Bramble, guinea pigs, and all the other animals I have had the pleasure of keeping, God Bless them all.

To my mum, Lisa (to my dad she will always be his very special lady), my dad David, to my nephew Oliver, Nan and Grandad Cook, Nan and Grandad Brown, Phyllis and Mollie, Lorna, Richard, Paul, Kathy, Nicky, Kevin, Keith, Paul, Ray, Mr and Mrs Harbour, Aunty Glenny. To my present and past work colleagues, friends, fellow conservationists, thank you, and God bless you all.

This world would not be a nice place if I had not had the privilege of meeting these people, and having the friendship and unconditional love from those beautiful animals, God Bless you all.

With thanks to Austin Macauley Publishers and the organisations for the pictures of the animals, forests, cloud forests, oceans etc, showing in particular pictures of the elephants, rhinos, leopards, lions, bison, tigers, lemurs, dolphins, whales, seals, wolves, sharks, manta rays, wild horses, penguins, birds of prey, parrots, badgers, gorillas, apes, orangutans, birds of paradise, various bees, butterflies, frogs, insects, lizards, orchids, cactus etc.

For the photos of the Yorkshire Dales, Nepal and Thailand, the Yorkshire Regiment and the Dragoons, Gurkha Regiment, the mystic robed in grey and the Seeress robed in blue.

A dedication to the amazing singer Michael Jackson and his wonderful song 'The Earth Song' and Axtu Leman for his Peruvian song, a fitting tribute to our wonderful and endangered wildlife, the amazing people, the domesticated animals, and the plant diversification, habitats across the world. I pray that 2020 is the year that we all can make a difference and help save our precious world, after all it is our only home.

To those wonderful composers and singers whose songs are in the book, a fitting tribute to them, thank you.

A very special dedication to a very special man, wildlife conservationist, Sir David Attenborough, a very big thank you for what you have achieved in helping us all to help save our amazing wildlife, the wonderful habitats of the world, and the amazing people who care for them.

Christopher Hayes-Brown

LADY VISIT TO NEPAL AND THE FAR EAST

AUSTIN MACAULEY PUBLISHERS™
LONDON · CAMBRIDGE · NEW YORK · SHARJAH

A CIP catalogue record for this title is available from the British Library.

ISBN 9781398412323 (Paperback)
ISBN 9781398412330 (ePub e-book)

www.austinmacauley.com

First Published (2021)
Austin Macauley Publishers Ltd
25 Canada Square
Canary Wharf
London
E14 5LQ

Acknowledgements

My wonderful mum, dad, grandparents, nephew Oliver, to my fantastic friends, Sam, Richard, Jamie, Rachel, Mike, Lorna, Andreas, Charlie, the staff at Pets at Home, Hart Vets, a big thank you to Austin Macauley Publishers, the police especially Thames Valley Police and the rescue services, my friends in the martial arts, especially Richard and family, the various animal organisations across the world, Oxfordshire Animal Sanctuary, Blue Cross, the local shop keepers and businesses, PDSA, WWF, BBONT, the RSPB, RHS, Orchid Society of Great Britain, Burnham Nurseries, Orchid Alchemy, Laneside Hardy Orchids, Phasmid Study Group, Hardy Orchid Society, Marie Curie, NSPCC, The War Veterans associations across the world, including NAVVET, the various military regiments and support services, including the Yorkshire Regiment and Gurkha Regiment, To His Holiness Pope Francis and other religious faiths, Buckingham and Preston Bissett Nurseries, Brackley Antiques, and the amazing medical organisations, thank you all.

To all the readers who have enjoyed reading my books, I have enjoyed writing them, a special thank you to you all.

After the end of World War Two, it was now time to rebuild the villages, towns, cities destroyed in the war across Europe. To bring harmony, peace to the human race, who have suffered such casualties, but we must also remember the animals who gave up their lives, the unforgotten heroes, the animals who took part and made the ultimate sacrifice, the horses, ponies, donkeys, dogs, pigeons, hawks, cats, and the many other species of animals who have also played their part in those wars, for they gave up their lives so that we all could live in a better world.

But we must also never forget the wonderful armed forces and support services from across the world who gave up their lives, such as, the British, European, Mediterranean, Australian, African, Nepalese, Canadian, USA, West Indies, Indian, and numerous other countries that helped during the first and second World Wars so that the many may live, claiming in the end millions of human lives in the name of freedom and from the evils of tyranny.

Now our big challenge is to start to value our precious world from further destruction, those that share this world with us, and now the challenges for wildlife conservation to help save the amazing habitats, the creatures that live within, such as the rain forests, cloud forests, deserts, the grass plains, woods, forests, swamps, heathlands, rivers, seas, the artic, to name but a few precious environments.

2020 will be a challenging year ahead after the terrible fire across the world that claimed human lives, but also millions of animals' lives, and now the human race has another treat on its hands, the coronavirus, which is claiming thousands of human beings' lives.

It is now, at this point in time, as a human race that we can work together to find a cure for this disease, but also change our world for the better, to make it safer for all to live on. To be more responsible, caring, good custodians, and compassionate to other humans, and more so to our fellow animals, since we are, after all, part of the animal kingdom. Let us respect and care for the amazing habitats, after all, this wonderful planet earth that we live in, is our only home.

So please, let 2021 be the year we make these changes for us and for the future generations, the amazing wildlife and domesticated animals, we, after all, owe it to them too, and finally, the diverse plant life across the globe, the lungs of the earth.

This powerful story tells of the amazing adventures of Lisa, her son David and their young black and tan female medium haired German shepherd dog called Lady, who are given a great opportunity to travel to Nepal on a two year conservation programme, which will be full of wonder, emotions, unconditional dedication, sacrifice, soul searching, sometimes tearful sights, but above all rewarding with challenges that lay ahead, and extreme dedication of the people who they share their adventures with, in particular the Nepalese, and Asian people, who care for their wonderful country's habitat and wildlife within. A story that will touch your very heart and soul, and as for the people, it will change their lives forever.

The story begins in January 1956, in a small peaceful and friendly Yorkshire village called Inkford. A village where the villagers always help each other out, truly a caring community. The love and affection they have for one another, where the kettle is always on the boil with a welcoming warm smile.

Lisa, the beloved partner to her late soul mate and partner David, and their wonderful young son, called David Christopher Brown, who inherited his father's wonderful looks, that mop of brown hair on his head, and deep blue eyes, but not forgetting the most precious thing that holds both of them together, Lady, a female black and tan German shepherd dog, related to the old Lady, much loved and who will never be forgotten.

Lisa, over time, has tried to come to terms with the loss of both David and Lady, who both served the king and country during the Second World War, but what they both did to help the community after the war, holds no bounds.

For David's family, the villagers and his army friends, for them to have known David and lady, two wonderful characters and the impact they had on them.

It was nothing for David and Lady to undertake such tasks, such as, delivering food, clothing and doing odd jobs, raising money for good causes, visiting the school children, assist in search and rescue, as well as the daily chores on the family farm, was truly amazing and touched hearts.

Now Lisa, their son David and young Lady are now living together on David's parent's farm called 'The Willow Tree', which has been owned by the Brown family for many generations; the name refers to the willow trees that grow along the banks of the stream that eventually runs into a small river travelling through some of the farmland.

The farm has about 50 acres of prime land, which is mainly used to grow various cereal crops, pastures for the dairy herds, the hay meadows for various grazing animals, the cattle, the sheep, the goats, and shire horses, there is also a large wood with native trees, some are used for coppicing and a beautiful wild flower meadow that attracts the various insect pollinators, such as the bees and butterflies. In the summer you can hear the grasshoppers and crickets. On the ant moulds you will see the common lizards and in the damp areas if you're lucky you may come across slow worms.

There's a large orchard for the growing of brambly apples, coxes (eating apples), conference pears with opal, Victoria and greengage plums, merry weather damsons, large fruiting quinces, sloes, as well as cobs and hazelnuts. Adjoining the orchard, is a large area for the growing a variety of fruit bushes, including, yellow gooseberries, red, white and black currents, raspberries, strawberries, loganberries, tayberries, varieties of brassica vegetables, various root crops, such as potatoes, onions, carrots, swedes and parsnips. Finally, an area set aside for growing cut flowers, such as dahlias, sweet peas, chrysanthemums, corn flowers, corn cockle, larkspur, bells of Ireland.

The farm itself has a number of outbuildings including stables, a 'dairy' with an area for the production of milk, butter, cheese, and cream. Nearby, large barns to house the hay and straw barns, cereal barns, with barns for the overwintering of the livestock. Pig sties with grounds, set aside for the pigs to roam freely within, and a plot of land near the orchard for the chickens, ducks and geese to roam freely. There is also a large pond for the ducks and geese to paddle freely.

The farmhouse has a large back garden with a wildlife pond, which attract the newts, toads and frogs, as well as the dragonflies and damselflies, and a large greenhouse for the growing of various plants, there are herbaceous borders filled with various types of cottage plants, including cowslips, primroses, irises, geraniums, lupins, poppies, asters, delphiniums, ox eye daisies, soapworts, daffodils, lilies of the valley, crocuses, tulips, various sun flowers, which the wild birds love, old fashioned marigolds, violets, dead nettles, violas, larkspurs, sweet peas, sweet rockets, peonies, delphiniums, golden rods, sedums, foxgloves, phloxes. Then there are various shrubs, including mahonia, winter flowering elegans, mock oranges, ribes, wintersweet shrubs, dwarf pines, rhododendrons, shrub honeysuckles, assorted rocky plants in an odd ceramic sink, various types of herbs such as mint, rosemary, lavender, thyme, sage, parsley, old fashioned scented roses including musk, hybrid teas, Persian herbs, and a very special rose called Black Baccarra, a very dark rose, honeysuckles, jasmines, and a Japanese blue flowering wisteria growing along the side of the farmhouse.

The other side of the farm is an open woodland with a mix of beech, oak, holly, privet, pines, ash, willow, birch, dog roses, rowan, sloe etc. In the spring, the forest floor is carpeted in wood anemones, in summer full of bluebells, cowslips, and primroses, in the late summer it is then full of the various flowering foxgloves, which the various bees truly love.

The farmhouse is furnished in various pine, elm, and oak furniture from dressers to pine furniture, chesterfield furniture, velvet curtains, old grandfather clocks in the hall and the sitting room, cast iron beds with handmade quilted covers, copper pans, pots etc. sheep skin rugs throughout the house, lead lighted windows, a welcoming fire in the sitting room and kitchen, the kettle always on the boil, the property is so inviting and welcoming to any visitor who may visit the Brown family.

It was a cold and frosty January morning, the snow was starting to fall, young David was watching the snow start to settle on his bedroom windowsill, curled up to him was Lady, keeping each other warm.

"Now now, David, you need to get washed and dressed, and then go down to the kitchen to have your breakfast with Lady," said his mum, Lisa, smiling at the pair of them.

"OK, Mum, I will see you downstairs in a few minutes," said David.

Lisa then kissed him on the head, and then said, "You remind meso much of your father, his good looks and that gentle smile. How proud he would be of you now," she then proceeded to make a fuss of Lady, and then said, "See you both downstairs."

Lisa then made her way downstairs to the kitchen to be greeted by the smell of fresh baked bread, a full breakfast fry-up laid on the table, also a selection of cereals, and mugs of piping hot tea. The Brown family were already seated at the table.

"Good morning, Lisa, I trust you had a good night's sleep," said Mr Brown.

"Thank you Mr Brown, we both slept well, and I hope you all had a good night's sleep too," said Lisa.

"Now, come and sit down, my love, I have laid a place for you and David at the table," said Mrs Brown.

As Lisa sat down, she then felt from under the table two wet noses, it was Layla and Troy, "Well good morning to you both, Layla and Troy, I suspect you are looking for any titbits," Lisa said, chuckling, then causing the rest of the family to laugh.

Then Troy and Layla's heads appeared, Troy looking up at Lisa and tilting his head, and Layla with those adoring, butter-would-not-melt eyes.

"Now now, you two let Lisa have her breakfast, you cannot help but love you two," said Mrs Brown, with a gentle smile, and deep affection for the two dogs, both carrying the traits of their mother Lady.

Then, all of a sudden, the door leading to upstairs opened, Lady ran out to be joined by Layla and Troy, by now making a big fuss of each other, then appears young David.

"Good morning, young man, I you had a good night's sleep, now come and join us for breakfast," said Mr Brown.

"I did, thank you, Grandad, I hope had my best mate curled up to me all night," said David.

Then David sat down, and tucked in to a hearty breakfast with his family, while Mrs Brown put three bowls of food for the three dogs who tucked in to it.

While the family sat around kitchen table having their breakfast and chattering about the chores that needed to be done on the farm, on the radio, the song being played by popular request was, 'where did our love go' by the Supremes, Mrs Brown humming away to the song.

Then the family finally finished breakfast, and Mr Brown, Oliver and Sam got up from the table, said their farewells, and left the kitchen heading off to milk the cows, then to start to feed the rest of the farm animals, checking that they were are all OK in the various barns, stables etc.

While Lisa started helping Mrs Brown in the kitchen, David, was now playing in the garden with the three dogs, all enjoying themselves playing in the snow, David giggling at them and then starting to throw snow balls into the air, which the dogs then started to catch in turn, then they started to roll in the snow with joy. Then David said, "you are so funny, you three, you make me laugh," as he then chuckled, and then smiled at them.

Mrs Brown then proceeded to open the side kitchen window looking out onto the garden, and said, "just look at the four of you, you will get wet in the snow, I see you, Troy, leading everyone astray, and you David, standing there giggling away," as she smiled at them, then closed the window.

"He reminds me so much of my son, David, when he was a little boy," Mrs Brown said, to Lisa, wiping a tear from her eye.

"We have the comfort and joy of knowing, that we had the chance of having two wonderful reminders of them both, in a young David and Lady. We are so lucky to have been given this," said Lisa, who then proceeded to give Mrs Brown a big hug, and then said further, "They will never be forgotten, they will always be in our hearts, they gave so much joy to us and those around, two very special beings who brought so much happiness into other people's lives."

"Now, you are absolutely right, and also they will always be watching over us all, from heaven above, and smiling down on their two prodigies, a younger David, and Lady, many people never have this chance, so yes we are so fortunate," said Mrs Brown, in a caring tone.

Then she said, "Well, let's get started with the house chores, and then we can start preparing the midday meals for the family," then they both proceeded to look outside into the garden again, watching David playing with the dogs, then Mrs Brown said, "Lisa, just look at them enjoying themselves."

Lisa then said, "Yes, it does touch your heart, such a picture of innocence, it is so wonderful to watch," trying to control her emotions.

Over the coming days, the snow had started to melt, and Lisa finally had a chance to go down to the village to lay some flowers on David's and Lady's grave with her son, and the new Lady.

It was a sunny morning when the three ventured down to the village, waving to some of the villagers as they passed by, and heading onwards towards the church graveyard. Then, finally arriving at their grave, Lisa bent down to lay the flowers by David and Lady's headstone, with tears rolling down her face, as music by Roy Orbison was playing from a radio in the distance.

David then grasping his mum by the hand said, "Please do not cry, Mummy, Daddy and his Lady are in heaven with the angels, and watching over us," in a reassuring voice.

With that, Lady then started nudging up to them both, in her own little way.

Lisa, then turned and kissed David on the forehead, and then stroked Lady.

Then Lisa got up, and then, all of a sudden, they saw seated by an oak tree, were the ghosts of David and Lady. David then said softly, "Please do not cry, my love, we will always be with you, like a guardian angel, I will always love you, our young son David Christopher, who I never had the chance to see born, and the so beautiful younger Lady."

Then the ghosts vanished, the three stunned at what they saw, young David then looked up to mother, and said, "You see mummy they are watching over us, and have spoken, daddy was a very handsome man, and Lady very similar to the Lady sitting next to both of us now."

"Yes, he was David, and you remind me so much of him, and the younger Lady has inherited the first Lady's looks and temperament," said Lisa.

Lady then looking up at them both and shaking her head, puzzled also at what she had just seen.

Lisa then said, "Now, let us walk back to visit Grandad Cook at the forge, and give the couple of carrots that Nan gave us for Jess the horse," with a gentle smile.

As they walked through the village, greeting the villagers as they passed by them, eventually, they arrived at the forge, David ran straight over to greet his grandad with a big hug, the radio in the forge was playing, 'Stand by Me' sung by Ben E. King, then followed by 'O Holy Night' (Andre Reiu) sung by a world-famous choir backed with female and lead male singers.

"Well, how is my grandson? And what a big hug David has for his grandad, and how is our Lady?" said Mr Cook. Lady by now was sitting down wagging her tail with excitement and then tilting her head from side to side trying to listen to the words spoken, as he, patted Lady on the head, and then said, "You're so loveable lady, oh and a paw shake, thank you."

Then he said, "Now then, how is my beautiful daughter?" Then giving her a kiss on the cheek and a huge hug, and he then said, "it will get better, my love, as time goes by, I can see you have been crying, now chin up, love, it does break my heart to see you like this. I know what it is like, when I lost your wonderful mother, we always will have those wonderful memories to treasure, and time is a great healer, my love, now, come on all of you, let us go into the kitchen, warm up by the fireplace, with a cup of tea and a piece of homemade cake," he said.

They then all proceeded to the kitchen where they stayed for about an hour. During that time, David suddenly got up and said, "May I go over and give Jess the two carrots?"

Then Grandad said, "Of course David, I think Jess is looking forward to seeing you," then David went over to the stable followed by Lady, wagging her tail from side to side, where Jess was now peering out from the stable door.

He then gently stroked Jess on the muzzle, and said, "How are you Jess?" Jess replied with nay, he then gave her the carrots one after the other, as she munched away with content, while Lady just looked up at them both.

Then he said, "Bye bye, Jess, we will see you again soon," then he proceeded to play ball with Lady in the small garden at the back of the house, while Lisa was chatting to her dad keeping him up to date on the happenings up at the farm.

Meanwhile, back at the farm, some letters had just been delivered by Tom the postman, "Hello, Mrs Brown," he said, and then was greeted by Layla and Troy with his ball in his mouth, egging Tom to play with him.

"Well, Tom," said Mrs Brown, "I see they never miss a trick when you visit us. Oh, Troy, you want to play ball with Tom and Layla." Troy looking up with those soft brown eyes, and Layla next to him tilting her head to catch the words being spoken.

"Well, OK Layla and Troy, I will play ball for a couple of minutes with you, then I must get on with my rounds," said Tom.

Throwing the ball around the garden, with Layla and Troy racing around after it in excitement.

Next thing you know Mr Brown with his two sons, Oliver and Sam, arrived at the garden from completing their morning chores around the farm.

"I see you are keeping Layla and Troy active chasing the ball around, Tom," said Mr Brown.

"Hello Mr Brown, Oliver and Sam, yes, they both love playing ball, I just do not know where they get the energy from," said Tom, then he said, "well I must go now, have a good day all of you."

"You too, Tom," said Mr and Mrs Brown, while the two boys were now playing ball with Layla and Troy.

Tom then left the garden and started to proceed down the farm track heading back towards the village.

"Now, come on all of you, in to the Kitchen for a refreshing cup of tea, and some buttered crumpets," said Mrs Brown.

With that they all headed off in to the kitchen, followed by two now panting and tired dogs.

"Well, you two, here are two bowls of cold water for you two to drink," said Mrs Brown, and with that both Layla and Troy started lapping up the water, and then proceeded to lay by the kitchen fireplace on a warm sheepskin rug, and then fell fast asleep.

"I see we have a fair bit of post, Mum," said Mr Brown in an inquisitive tone, as they all then sat around the kitchen table.

"Yes, and there is an air mail envelope addressed to Lisa, sent from the post mark in Nepal," said Mrs Brown, with interest.

"Lisa will be back soon to open it, is there is anything else of interest, Mum?" said Mr Brown.

"A bill for the repairs to the tractor, from Mr Tompkins, a letter from Aunt Lottie sending her kind regards to us all from her recent trip to Venice, where she had a wonderful time, you have to read the letter later," then she said, "the latest farmers newsletter, and my knitting patterns booklet," said Mrs Brown.

After a while, Sam, Oliver and Mr Brown got up.

"Thanks mum for the midday meal, that will keep us all going until tea time"; said Mr Brown, then pausing, he then said, "Oliver and Sam, let's check the cattle and the sheep on the high pastures to see if they are okay for the night, then we need to see to the hen coups, the roofing needs re-felting, and then we will need make sure the animals in the barns and outhouses are bedded down, fed and watered for the night, a lot to do while the weather is on our side,".

"See you later," said the boys to Mum.

"See you later, and keep warm all of you, especially up on the hills at this time of the year, it can still be quite chilly at this time of year," said Mum.

Then they left the kitchen and started heading off towards the hill fells, Sam and Oliver giggling with each other, with Mr Brown just smiling at them.

"Well, I see, Layla and Troy, you are both out for the count, bless you both, a picture of content," said Mrs Brown, and then said to herself, "well I must finish washing up the pots and then get the log baskets and coal scuttle filled for the night, before I can start preparing the evening meal."

Troy then looked up at Mrs Brown, tilting his head from side to side, then went back to sleep, while Layla rolled over on her back, then finally cuddling up to Troy, "I do know you two certainly have a good life," said Mrs Brown with a smile.

Mrs Brown proceeded with the kitchen chores while listening to an Elvis song on the radio, 'Can't Help Falling in Love', followed by 'Just One Look' sung by Doris Troy, and singing to herself, while she was working, wiggling her hips to the music.

Meanwhile, back at the forge, Lisa then got up from the kitchen chair, and said, "Well we must now start getting back to the farm," then giving her father a kiss on the cheek, and a big hug, "love you, Dad," she said.

"Now, Lisa, remember what I have said, chin up, remember the good times and fond memories you had with David and Lady, cherish your wonderful son, and the younger version of Lady, they will always be by your side, finally out of sadness there will be joy, my love," said dad, then proceeded to give Lisa a hug and a kiss on her cheek.

Then he said, "Well, my special grandson, give your old grandad a big hug before you go away," David then raced over to his grandad and cuddled him tightly.

David then said, "Love you and we will see you again soon."

Then Lady proceeded to brush up against Mr Cook, "Well we cannot forget you, Lady, now," giving her a cuddle and she reciprocated by giving him her paw, "thank you Lady."

"Now, take care all of you, and see you soon," said Mr Cook, and waving as they started to walk up the road, David and Lisa turning to wave back to him, while Lady barked to say goodbye in her own little way.

After a while they were all making their way back up towards the farm. Lisa could see from a distance Oliver and Sam driving the cows down the hill ready for the evening milking, while Mr Brown was mending one of the gates.

Finally, Lisa, David and Lady arrived at the farmhouse, opened the kitchen door to be greeted by Layla and Troy, who then started to make a fuss of them all, and in particular Lady.

Once inside the kitchen, they took off their coats, then Lisa said, "Now, David, please go and sit in the sitting room with your comic and the dogs, and keep warm, while I go and help Nan, with filling the log baskets, and the coal scuttle."

Lisa then proceeded to the yard where Mrs Brown was in the outhouse starting to fill up one of the log baskets with logs, "Here, Mum, let's help you," said Lisa.

"Thank you Lisa, did you have a nice time with your dad?" said Mrs Brown.

"Thank you, yes, it still catches me when visiting David's and Lady's grave to place the bunch of flowers. Young David is never going to be given the chance to grow up with his father," said Lisa with a tear in her eyes.

"Now, come on, pet, time is a great healer. OH my, just forgot, Lisa, there is letter for you, from Nepal. Now come let's finish filling these log baskets, and then fill the coal scuttle, we can then sit and have a hot cup of tea, the kettle is on the boil," said Mrs Brown.

After finally bringing in the log baskets and coal scuttle into the kitchen, to be placed by the sitting room and the kitchen area.

"I will make the tea, Lisa, the letter is by kitchen dresser, now, please have a seat, I will bring the pot of tea over, oh where is David?" said Mrs Brown.

"He is fast asleep on the chesterfield, with Lady by his side and Layla and Troy fast asleep on the sheep skin rug, what a picture," said Lisa.

"Well, Lisa, I am so eager to hear who the letter is from" said Mrs Brown, excitedly

Lisa proceeded to open the letter, "It is from one of David's old army comrades, Jake Williams, he is working in Nepal as a wildlife conservationist and is flying over here to collect various provisions, and would like to visit us at the farm," said Lisa intriguingly.

"Well, that is some good news, Lisa, when is he coming over?" said Mrs Brown with interest.

"He says he will be in England on the 24th January, weather permitting, and he is bringing two people with him, he will not say who," said Lisa, and then said, "Well, mum, and who could they be? I am puzzled."

"Well, Lisa, I suggest we will have to get the spare room ready for Jake and his companions to stay" said Mrs Brown, then she said with excitement., "this is like a Miss Marple mystery, I cannot wait to meet them all,"

"Oh my, Lisa, the 24th is only a couple of days away, we have a lot to prepare before then, do we know what time he will arrive at the station?" said Mrs Brown.

"He says in the letter, all being well, he should arrive at the station late afternoon," said Lisa.

"While David is asleep I suggest we both go and give a good airing to the spare room, it has two beds in it," said Mrs Brown.

So off they went upstairs, opened the windows to allow fresh air into the room.

Mrs Brown then went to the airing cupboard to bring some sheets and blankets, then she said, "Lisa, can you carry some pillows for me?"

While this was going on, Mr Brown and his two sons finally entered the kitchen to find Layla and Troy fast asleep on the kitchen rug, and David with Lady cuddled up on the chesterfield in the sitting room.

"Oliver and Sam, make yourselves a cup of tea, and pour one out for me, please, while I go and find Mum and Lisa," said Dad.

Mr Brown made his way upstairs to find Mrs Brown and Lisa in the spare room, "What is going on?" said Mr Brown, with intrigue.

"Dad, Lisa is going to have some visitors coming over from Nepal on the 24th January, so we are busy making up the spare room," said Mrs Brown. She then said, "Now, Dad, go downstairs and warm up by the fire, we will join you all in a short while, after we have finished up here."

Mr Brown proceeded back downstairs to join his sons for a cup of tea.

That evening, they all sat around the kitchen table enjoying macaroni and cheese, homemade Victoria cake and mugs of tea, discussing the forthcoming visitors to the farm.

The days rolled by quickly, and the Brown family started to get the farmhouse ready for their visitors.

After a hearty breakfast, and after the morning farm chores had been completed, the family then all got ready for the big day.

Mr Brown then said "Well, Lisa and I will go down to collect Jake and his companions from the railway station, now, boys, stay and help Mum, and look after young David, and the dogs."

Then, both Mr Brown and Lisa left the farmhouse, waving goodbye as they left, and then heading towards the yard, were they both climbed onto the cart, "well, off we go now, Major, walk on" said Mr Brown.

Lisa shed tears as the memories came flooding back as it reminded her that it was the beloved Major, the Shire horse, who David and Lady were delivered by to their final resting place at the church, some years ago.

"Now, Lisa, dry your eyes, now, my pet, we must put a brave face on for your guest," said Mr Brown in a gentle and kind tone to his voice.

As they rode through the village, villagers stood to wave them on, finally, they arrived at the railway station.

Mr Brown helped Lisa off the cart, and then they rode Major to the post.

They then proceeded to the station platform, and then sat down to wait for the train, it seemed like hours had past, a very special song came across the station radio, 'Slipping Through My Fingers' (from Mamma Mia), Lisa sat, tears rolling down her face.

"Oh Lisa, I know the pain and suffering you must be feeling, not a day goes past that I don't think of David and Lady, and shed a tear, please do not mention this to Mum," said Mr Brown.

Lisa then proceeded to hug Mr Brown, "I so miss them and it breaks my heart. Will a special love ever appear to me," said Lisa, as the tears rolled down her eyes.

"My love, keep your chin up, in your heart and soul they will always be with you, and like guardian angels they are watching over us now," said Mr Brown, brushing the tears from his eyes.

Then, all of a sudden, they heard the whistle of the steam train heading towards the station.

The station master, Mr Griffith, prepared to receive the incoming train, white smoke billowing from the train's funnel, then the train finally came to a halt at the platform.

Then Lisa and Mr Brown stood up.

Mr Griffith then said, "Welcome to Inkford station", as the carriage doors then open, several people started to disembark from their carriages.

Then, in the distant a young man started to walk forward holding the hands of two little boys, followed by a porter with two suitcases.

Lisa then nervously approached the young man, and said, "Are you by chance Jake?"

He then replied, "Yes I am, and these are my two sons, Benjamin and Omar."

"Now, say hello to Miss Cook," said Jake.

"Please, all of you, call me Lisa," she said.

Jake then proceeded to give Lisa a big hug, and then said, "I am so sorry for your loss, David and Lady were so special to me, I will never forget them both."

Then the two boys took turns to shake Lisa's hands and then they said, "Hello, Lisa," in a very gentle voice.

"Oh, my manners, this is Mr Brown, David's father," said Lisa.

"Hello, Mr Brown, I remember you when we disembarked from the train arriving back from the war, and also those happy times we all spent on your farm with David, Lady, Mrs Brown, Oliver and Sam," said Jake.

Mr Brown then said, "Is your wife not with you?" as they all started to walk back towards the cart were Major was tethered.

"I am sorry, no, my wonderful wife Kira died a year ago from a brain haemorrhage, it has been distressing for me and our two boys, who miss their mother so much," said Jake emotionally trying to hold back his tears as best he could, and not to be seen crying in front of his sons.

"I am so sorry, Jake," said Mr Brown, while the song 'Cora' was being played on the station radio (Last of the Mohicans).

Lisa wiping a tear from her eyes, after hearing the sad news from Jake, then proceeded to help the two boys onto the cart, then sat next to them.

Then Jake put the two suitcases onto the cart and then thanked the porter.

Then Mr Brown proceeded to untether Major from the post.

Jake and Mr Brown then proceeded to climb on-board the front of the cart, while Lisa sat at the back with Benjamin and Omar looking very nervous and afraid, then Mr Brown said, "Walk on Major," as they proceeded to leave the railway station heading back towards the farm.

On their journey back Lisa started to discuss with Benjamin and Omar about their journey from Nepal, what it was like and if they are looking forward to spending time on the farm. Their response was touching, she could see from their faces, they missed their mother, but also were tired from their long journey.

Omar and Benjamin started to cry and said together, "we miss our mummy."

"Now, now, my loves," said Lisa in a sad voice, hugging both of them, and then she said, "we will soon be at the farm, my family, and the farm animals are looking forward to seeing you all, especially my son, David, with Lady, Layla and Troy," in a manner of a mother' love, and understanding what they are going through.

Jake then turned and said in a gentle voice, "Omar, and Benjamin, cheer up, I love you both so much, it breaks my heart to see you both like this. I miss your mother so much, your mummy will always be with you both, and will always love you, even though she is now in heaven, she will always watch over you all," said Jake as he wiped tears from his eyes, and then said tearfully, "Oh Kira, I so do miss you, my love."

(The song 'Away from You', from Pompeii).

Mr Brown turned and said, "Now, Jake, cheer up, my friend, it is so very hard when losing loved ones, now chin up lad, and welcome to our home, which I hope you all will treat as your home."

Mr Brown then said, "Well, my friends, we have arrived at the farm," Mrs Brown was already outside the farmhouse to greet them.

They all disembarked from the cart, then Mr Brown lead Major and the cart back into the stables.

"Mrs Brown, may I introduce you to Jake and his two sons, Benjamin and Omar," said Lisa.

Mrs Brown then said, "Welcome, Jake, Benjamin and Omar, please, come into the farmhouse, warm yourselves up by the kitchen fire, I have the kettle on the boil ready to make the tea, there is also some home lemonade, hot buttered crumpets, fruit trifle, and homemade cakes."

They all then entered the kitchen to be greeted by the warmth coming from kitchen fire, the smell of freshly baked bread and cakes all laid out on the kitchen table.

Lady, Layla and Troy raced over to greet them with licks, then Oliver, Sam and David appeared.

"Jake, Benjamin and Omar, these are my two sons, Oliver and Sam, and my grandson, David," said Mrs Brown.

Then she said, "Come now, let's sit down and enjoy the spread laid out for you all to enjoy."

Then, all of a sudden, the kitchen door opened, Mr Brown entered, went over to the kitchen sink and washed his hands, and said, "Well, Mum you truly have provided an excellent spread for us all to enjoy," said Mr Brown.

"Come now, enjoy the food, you must so hungry after such a long journey," said Mrs Brown, as they all started to tuck in, with Lady, Layla and Troy watching out for anything to drop on the floor.

"Now, now, Troy, Layla and Lady you have all been fed, your eyes are bigger than your belly," said Mrs Brown with a smile.

This caused the children to start laughing at the sights of the three dogs, with their butter-would-not-melt-eyes.

Mrs Brown then said, "Now, that's better, my loves. The dogs have made you all laugh, especially Lady looking as she has not been fed, trying to give you her paw as well, Troy Tilting his head, and as for those adorable eyes of Layla. What characters they have, you now have some new friends."

As they settled down, enjoying their tea and discussing their day, after an hour, Lisa then said, "David, I think it is time for your bed, young man, say goodnight to everyone," he proceeded to kiss his nan, granddad, Lisa, Oliver and Sam and then shook hands with Jake, Benjamin and Omar.

"I shall be upstairs in a minute, David," said Lisa.

"Goodnight," said David in a gentle voice, as he left with Lady following him upstairs.

Lisa then got up and said to Jake, "If you like, I will show you all to your rooms."

"Well, that is the cue for my two sons to go to bed, come on, sleepy heads, and now thank everyone for the lovely food, Benjamin and Omar," said Jake.

"Thank you," said Omar and Benjamin, in a gentle voice and then yawning, both so tired after their long day, as Jake proceeded to take them upstairs to bed.

"Good night to you all and sweet dreams," said Mr and Mrs Brown. While the radio was playing 'I have a dream' sung by Abba.

"I cannot believe this, Layla and Troy have got up, wagging their tails and then they have followed Jake, Omar and Benjamin to bed," Oliver said smiling, and then chuckled with his brother Sam.

"Well, this is a first, you just have to laugh at them, but boy do you love them," said Sam laughing.

"Well, it will give them some company, I hope they do not mind having the two dogs with them," said Mrs Brown.

"I am sure they will be OK, Mum," said Mr Brown, starting to laugh, then said, "Sam and Oliver, you have lost your two furry friends for the night."

"Now, Dad, do not tease, dogs are clever animals they can pick up unusual human behaviour and emotions as we all, you know? In this case, the two boys needed some comfort," said Mrs Brown.

"Well, it's been a long day. I suggest that we all have a good night's sleep, as we all have a busy day tomorrow," said Mr Brown, starting to yawn.

Then, Mrs Brown went upstairs followed by Dad and the two boys, then Mrs Brown turned to them and said in a quiet voice, "Just look at that, a picture of happiness and content, Jake with his two sons next to him, with Layla and Troy by either's side, truly melts your heart."

Then as they moved on to the next room, to then see David and Lady cuddled up to each other, "I see Lady has David's panda under her paw, what a sight," said Mrs Brown, with a smile.

Then Mrs Brown and Mr Brown said, "Well, goodnight Sam and Oliver, and thank you both for welcoming our new guests."

Sam and Oliver, then said in a soft voice, "Goodnight Mum, and goodnight Dad," and then headed off to their bedroom.

Next morning eventually came, the sun shining through the kitchen window, while Mr Brown and the two boys were undertaking the early morning farm chores, Mrs Brown was starting to prepare breakfast, listening to the song '(Your Love Keeps Lifting Me)Higher and Higher', and then followed, by 'Unchained Melody' on the radio.

While outside David, Benjamin and Omar were playing in the garden with the dogs, laughing and giggling.

In the sitting room, Jake then suddenly turned to Lisa and said, "Well, we have not long arrived here, the Yorkshire hospitality has been as always so wonderful, but we will need to travel back to Nepal soon, it would be an honour if you, David and Lady could come back with us. I have the necessary paperwork, please say yes."

"We would love it, it would a dream for us to see another country, but the sad bit is I will miss leaving the family," said Lisa, hesitantly, but surprised at the same time.

"We would be away for only a couple of years undertaking a new conservation project I am working with the Nepalese and Indian authorities, you will all love it, and it would be great for Omar and Benjamin, then we can return back here to your family, if you want? I do understand about your close ties with your family, it never is easy, but this is a once in a lifetime opportunity," said Jake, with those soft brown eyes, looking at her.

"OK, Jake, we will need to mention it to the family here and then we will need to see my father to inform him of our intentions," said Lisa.

Then during breakfast the conversation was raised.

Mr Brown then said, "Lisa we would be so happy for you all, it would be a wonderful experience, yes, I cannot say we won't miss you all, but this is a chance for you all to see the world, and for such good cause, for Lady a new experience."

"After breakfast, if you all do not mind, I will take Jake, Benjamin, Omar and David to see my dad," said Lisa.

"Lisa, I will prepare a basket of farm produce for your Dad, send him our love, he is always welcome up here," said Mrs Brown, in a gentle tone to her voice.

"Well, back to work now, Oliver and Sam, I will get Major harnessed up to the cart, ready for your ride down to the village," said Mr Brown.

"Thanks Mr Brown," said Jake.

While Lisa and Jake then started putting the coats on the boys, saying goodbye to Mrs Brown, as they left the kitchen, then climbing on-board the horse and cart, then they headed off, down the farm track towards the village.

Finally they reached the village, there was Mr Cook working in the forge, while Jess was peering out from the stable at them.

Lisa then tethering Major to the post outside the forge.

Then, David raced to his grandad to give him a big hug, "well, it's great to see you David," said Mr Cook, and then said, "miss you, little boy" then planted a kiss on his forehead.

"Hello Dad, may I introduce David's old army comrade, Jake, with his two sons, Benjamin and Omar," also Mrs Brown sends her love," said Lisa, as she handed him the basket of goodies, and then gave him a kiss on his cheek.

"It's a pleasure to meet you all, and then shaking their hands in turn "come, let's go to the kitchen, the kettle is on the boil, so let us have a nice cup of tea and sit by the range, it's been a busy morning for me at the forge making new horse shoes for Lady MacCready's horses," said Mr Cook.

Then proceeding to the kitchen, they all sat down with a piping hot cup of tea and a piece of cake that Mrs Brown had provided in the basket of goodies.

"Well, how is everything been going at the farm Lisa, and Jake? What brings you over to this side of the world?" said Mr Cook.

"Well, Mr Brown is busy as usual at the farm in preparation for the arrival of the new baby animals to be born in the spring, and as for Jake, he has come over to ask if David, Lady and me can go back to Nepal for two years, to assist in the conservation program for the people and the wildlife," said Lisa excitedly, but also nervous about the response from her father.

"Lisa, I think this is the chance you have been waiting for, to see the world, take it and enjoy it, it's an experience of a lifetime, it will do you, David and Lady, good," said Mr Cook.

Then he said, "Lisa, I think this is what you have been waiting for, my love."

"I promise, Mr Cook, that I will look after them all, they will enjoy Nepal and India. The people there are so friendly, the wildlife is wonderful, and my two boys will love to have Lisa, David and Lady with them," said Jake.

"So, what does the conservation work entail, Jake?" said Mr Cook.

"The main objective is to help and protect the wildlife especially the snow leopards, and tigers, create a large protected reserve to be patrolled by the native people with specially trained dogs, and also to educate the local people to live in harmony with the wonderful creatures, which, at present, are being unnecessarily killed by poachers and their parts used for medicines," he then paused and then said, "we will need to leave in a couple of days' time," said Jake in a sad tone.

"I cannot understand how animals can cure illnesses with their bodily parts etc. but I do know that plants can, well, good on you lad, these creatures have a right to live on the planet as well as us, I am all for this, now keep me posted on all that is going on in Nepal, and let me have some photos to see please." He then turns to Lisa, then Mr Cook said, "Now, pet, look after yourselves and promise you'll write. David, enjoy yourself and learn the ways of the world, it will put you in good stead in later life, and as for you, Lady, my wonderful girl, protect these wonderful creatures from harm", he said as he stroked Lady on the head, she reciprocated by giving him per paw, "Lady, you and all in this room are so special," said a tearful Mr Cook.

"Come one now, Dad, I shall cry. We will be back here in two years' time," said Lisa, as they all got up to say goodbye to Mr Cook.

The radio was then playing 'We Have All the Time in the World' sung by Louis Armstrong, Mr Cook giving them all a big hug. Then he said, "I shall see you all at the train station," wiping the tears from his eyes as he waved goodbye to them, as they headed up through the village, back to the farm.

On their way back, they passed Lady MacCready and her head gamekeeper riding the pony and trap, who then suddenly stopped to say hello.

"Lisa, how are you all? I am off to see your father to collect the horseshoes. Oh, by the way, you may have noticed in the back is Honey, the Labrador, and she has made friends with Zeus, the black Labrador, owned by, you know, the ex-soldier Sergeant Marcus Forrester. He knew David while he was at the training camp," said Lady MacCready.

Then she said, "Zeus would follow Honey around the estate playing regularly, she is a little devil but you just have to love her with those puppy dog eyes. So, the next stop is for Honey to have a check-up by Mr Johnson the Vet. Well, nice to see you all, I must go, take care, all of you," said Lady MacCready in a hurried voice.

"Oh, by the way, nice to see you with Jake and his two sons Benjamin and Omar. He is a nice lad, Lisa, if you know what I mean" said Lady MacCready, then waved goodbye, and then they started heading off towards Mr Cook's forge.

"I can only assume that that is an approval from Lady MacCready, she has always been known for her open and frank views, but she's a great character in the village, and much loved by all, for her kindness. She's always willing to help others, especially during the war, but above all, for her love and passion for the wildlife, which also plays an important part in her life. Such a wonderful person," said Lisa trying not to blush with embarrassment, especially in front of Jake.

"Yes, a lady of character, but with a kind and caring heart, a very good friend to have, she certainly has a soft spot for you, Lisa," said Jake with a smile on his face, and knowing inside what Lady MacCready was referring to, then he gently brushed Lisa's shoulder, and then smiled at her.

Then as they rode through the village, the villagers would stop to wave to them.

Meanwhile Betty and Penny Fortisque, who had suddenly came out from their cottage just in time, to present Lisa a freshly baked fruit cake with buttercream.

"Hello, Lisa, this is for you and the family," said Penny, and then said, "I hope you all will enjoy it, especially the boys, Troy, Layla, and to one very special Lady," trying to hold her emotions as she was especially fond of the old Lady.

Then Betty said, "Well now, how is David and Lady? Oh where are my manners; nice to see you again, Jake, and what lovely sons you have, Benjamin and Omar. Welcome to Yorkshire," in a kind and gentle voice.

"Thank you, Betty and Penny, the cake will be well received by all. Oh, Mr Brown will be popping over tomorrow with your dairy produce as promised, take care both of you," said Lisa, they have always been like aunties to her, especially after her mother's death.

With that, David gave Betty and Penny a hug each, and then said, "thank you."

"Betty and Penny, it has been a long time since we last met, this time with my two sons, Benjamin and Omar, as you already know," said Jake.

The two boys then said in soft voice, "Nice to meet you both, take care," and then they smiled at Penny and Betty.

"Well, we must go now, and we will see you all soon. Betty and Penny, thank you again," said Lisa.

They all then waved goodbye to Penny and Betty, and headed off back to the farm.

Finally reaching the farm, they were greeted by Mrs Brown hanging out the washing on the line, "I hope you all have had a lovely day, now, come into the kitchen I have the kettle on the boil," said Mrs Brown.

Then the boys ran into the garden with Lady to be greeted by Layla and Troy, all playing happily with a ball while Lisa, Jake and Mrs Brown went into the kitchen for a cup of tea.

That evening they all sat around the kitchen table, tucking into homemade macaroni cheese, followed by jam roly-poly and custard, all enjoying the hearty meal, as usual the dogs were looking for any titbits that may go their way.

They then all sat around the sitting room, with a welcoming log fire throwing out the warmth into the room, dogs asleep on the sheepskin rug, and the children playing with some Britain toy soldiers, as the adults discussed the events of the day and the preparation for the Nepalese visit, the radio playing in the kitchen various George Formby songs, followed by a variety of Vera Lynn songs.

The day finally came, suitcases packed and everyone downstairs, saying their farewells, Mrs Brown in tears, Sam and Oliver hugging everyone, Layla and Troy as usual playing with Lady.

"Now, come on, Mum, they will all be back here in a couple of years, I have the horse and cart ready to take them to the railway station," said a sad Mr Brown, trying to hold back the tears himself from the family.

They all then left the kitchen, and finally Lisa, David, Lady, Jake, Benjamin and Omar were sitting on the cart, ready for Mr Brown to take them to the railway station.

"Mum, we will be back soon, now, boys look after Mum, and ensure the animals are bedded down for the day," said Mr Brown, now all wiping the tears from their eyes.

"Bye, bye Mrs Brown, bye, bye Nanny, Oliver and Sam, Layla and Troy," tears in their eyes welling up, little David waved goodbye with his panda's paw, Jake's sons huddled up to their dad with tears rolling down their little faces.

Then, with sounds of Layla and Troy barking in the kitchen, at one point Troy started to bay like a hound, their emotions running high by all.

Finally, the cart left the farm being pulled by Major the Shire horse's son called Samson, as they then headed towards the village.

To everyone surprise, the villagers had all come out to wave goodbye to them, again their emotions running high, some villagers in tears, then, finally they had arrived at the railway station to more villagers lining up at the railway platform.

They all disembarked from the cart, Mr Brown tethered Samson to the post and then followed the party to the platform, where the steam train was awaiting them.

There, on the platform, was Lady MacCready who proceeded to hug them all, and then presented a box to Lisa, tears in her eyes and then she said, "when you come back we need to talk, I will have a surprise for you, but for now I hope you all have a great time in Nepal, keep up the good work in the conservation project, and God bless you all, and come back safely," trying to hold back her emotions as best she could.

Lady MacCready then bent down to cuddle Lady, who then gave her, her paw, by now Lady MacCready had a tear rolling down her face, then she said, "I will especially miss you, my love, you have so many wonderful characteristics of the old Lady, we all so loved and cherished."

Then Mr Brown said his farewell, by now tears in his eyes, hugging each one, too choked to speak another word.

Mr Brown then hugging Lady, his tears dripping onto her fur, then said, "I love you all, now look after yourselves, and we will see you again soon," Lady as usual gave him her paw and a kiss on his face.

Then Mr Cook stepped forward to shake the hands of Jake, Benjamin, Omar, and then he started to cuddle Lisa, and David. Then finally, he bent down to cuddle Lady, then he stood up, trying to hold back his emotions. He then said, "Now Jake, please look after my daughter, grandson, and Lady," and then paused wiping the tears from his face, then said, "Until we all meet again", the expression on his face said it all.

Finally, Lisa and the party by now had boarded the train, the windows now wound down.

Lisa managed to say goodbye, with tears still streaming down her face and David waving goodbye with his panda's paw waving to everyone, his little face full of tears, Jake and his two boys also waving and tears in their eyes, and then came the sound of Lady howling, everyone by now on the platform was choked up with emotion.

Lady MacCready then proceeded those around her, while the rest of the villagers on the platform waved goodbye, as the train then started to move, with white smoke bellowing into the air from the funnel.

Lisa and everyone sat down, trying to comfort each other, as they travelled past the various villages, towns and countryside's, heading towards to the city of London.

Then to catch a taxi, and head off to London airport ready for the flight to Nepal.

There, waiting to greet them at the airport lobby was Rachel, Mike, Jamie, and Richard, fellow conservationists. As the taxi arrived at the airport entrance, they got out of the taxi, Jake thanking the driver for a smooth journey, the porters then started to collect their suitcases that are to be delivered onto the plane that would be flying them to Nepal.

Jake then turned to Lisa and said, "Those are my fellow conservationists in the lobby, let's go over to meet them."

"Lisa, and David, may I introduce you to Rachel, Jamie, Richard and Mike, and by the way this is Lady, then they all started exchanging greetings to each other, and making a fuss of the children, and Lady now with her green coat on with the words in white saying 'The Nepalese Wildlife Conservation Project'.

After a short while, the airport speakers announced over the tannoy, "Can all passengers for the Nepalese flight, please make their way to gate 4, ready to embark."

"Well, this is it," said Mike, "we are off, and I am truly looking forward to seeing the amazing wildlife."

"Yes," said Rachel, Jamie and Richard, "cannot wait to see in particular, the snow leopards, tigers, the wonderful wildlife and their habitats, and to meet the people of Nepal."

"Well, Lisa, boys and Lady, here we go," and then Jake said, to all, "I suggest as this is going to be a long journey we catch up on some sleep, and that goes for you too, Benjamin and Omar."

Lisa then said, "Will Lady be able to come with us to our seats?" as David then started yawning cuddling his panda, she then said, "oh, my sleepy little boy."

"Have no fear, all, an exception has been made for Lady to be with us, provided she lays down, and is kept under control, animals normally have to go to the cargo bay and put into a secured pen," said Jake.

Finally, they all boarded the plane and settled down for the long journey ahead, listening to the music being played on the radio, 'The God Speed Tracks' (from the time machine), followed by various other songs including 'Band of Gold' sung by Freda Payne, 'Please Don't Go' sung by KC and the Sunshine Band, 'I Can't Help Myself' sung by the Four Tops, 'Everlasting Love' from The Love affair, then 'Unchained Melody' by the Righteous Brothers, by then, they had all slowly fallen into a deep sleep. Lady fast asleep near David curled up with the panda toy he dropped onto the floor.

Eventually, after the long journey, they had finally arrived at Kathmandu airport, and airplane attendants started to gently wake them up, all by now yawning from a good long sleep, Lady then woke up and then handed David back his panda bear.

One of the airplane attendants then said, "thank you for flying with us on Nepalese Airways, can you all now please make your way to the exit door, down the stairs, and then proceed towards gate number 7, your luggage will be with you shortly there, ready for you to collect."

They all started to leave the plane heading towards gate 7 to be greeted by a group of local people who greeted them by singing and dancing a Maori type song (from the time machine), it truly lifted our spirits, then Benjamin, Omar and David started to join in the dancing, wiggling their hips, truly a sight to see, while Lady sat wagging her tail and tilting her head listening to the music.

This just touched all of their hearts, and Jake caught the moment on his camera, then smiling at the boys enjoying themselves.

Finally, they all moved into the airport lobby, to be greeted by their guides and Sherpas holding up a board with Nepalese Wildlife Conservation Project on it, Jake then said, "let me introduce you all to Vinh (Glory), Aarus (first ray of the sun), Dawa (the moon), Prashiwa (Lord Krishra), Tao (the sun)," they all exchanged greetings, then they made their way onto the green coach signed Nepalese Wildlife Conservation Project, with a picture of a snow leopard and tiger on both sides.

While on the coach, one of their guides called Aarus then said, " from the various Nepalese wildlife we may come across the two well-known animals that visitors love to see are the tiger and snow leopard high up in the mountains, but we also have blue sheep, yak, sloths, bears wolves, rhinos, wild buffalos called 'Arna'," then he paused and then said further, "the musk deer, monitor lizards, cobras, pythons, honey kites, vultures, eagles, black ibises, pheasants, storks, various butterflies, grasshoppers, mantis, glow worms (cheparo), various rhododendrons, poppies, pines, roses, Nepalese lilies, varieties of orchids ranging from pleiones, cymbidiums, coelogynes, vandas, dendrobiums, slipper orchids, to name but a few.

Aarus then said further, "The dogs we use for protecting the wildlife in the reserves are mainly German/Belgian shepherd dogs with some Labradors and Tibetan mastiffs, but also on your travels you will see a range of other different breeds of dogs and cats including the Tibetan cats, that are a bit like a Siamese, beautifully marked with those blue eyes."

Then he said further, "It is said when a temple priest dies he is reincarnated as a Tibetan cat. How true that is, who knows? But what a wonderful way to be remembered."

As we ascended up a hill we noticed coloured flags hanging up between two posts, Aarus then said, "These are prayer flags, offering prayers to Buddha, the different colours represent, blue for the sky, green for water, white for air and the wind, yellow for the earth and red for fire."

Lisa then turned to Jake and the team, then said, "I am just loving every minute and treasure every moment of this, what an amazing country."

Rachel then said, "Lisa, wait until you see where we are staying, you will love the beautiful surroundings, it is totally captivating."

Then as we turned the corner near to the sanctuary, a young man stepped out waving his hands, shouting "Please stop, please stop."

Vinh stopped the coach, Jake then left the coach, while we all waited, by now the children and Lady were awake still dazed after their long sleep.

Jake then said, "What is it my friend?"

"Please, please, help, a young tiger has been caught in a trap nearby, crying in pain," said the young man with tears in his eyes.

Jake then turned and said, "Mike, Richard, Rachel and Jamie please get the animal rescue kit with the cutters, hurry, there is a young tiger which has been caught in a trap, Lisa, please stay with the Sherpas and children on the coach, we will be back soon."

Then, in hot pursuit, they ran with the young man to a wooded area, hearing the howls of the tiger, deeply upsetting for all of them, at last, they saw the young tiger. Its paw caught tightly in the trap, struggling to try and release its paw, they could see tears around its eyes, the animal so distressed.

For them It was so emotional for all to see, especially to Rachel, whose eyes were welling up with tears, they were all shocked at what they saw, "How can anyone do this, they clearly have no respect for the wildlife, the suffering the trap causes and have no conscious for the world around, just selfless cruelty," said an emotional Vinh, totally stunned and shocked at the sight.

Jake then said, "Right, you all know what to do, I will sedate the tiger." The tiger then finally fell into a sleep, then Mike and Jamie opened the trap to release the tiger's paw, the process went reasonably well, but as always being cautious with wild animals like tigers. Rachel with Richard then proceeded to clean the paw, then treating with antibiotics and a painkiller and then carefully dressing the wound, while the young man watched full of tears, and then a crowd of people appeared from the nearby village to come and watch, looks of horror in their faces as they watched the young tiger laying still.

Jake then said, "Richard and Mike have a look around to see that there are no more traps nearby, if so disable and collect them, but be careful they are dangerous things, this trap will come back with us."

"We will be careful, Jake," said Richard and Mike.

With that, Richard and Mike left with a few young men from the village who volunteered to help them search for further traps.

"Right now, folks, we will need to carry the tiger carefully back to the coach, he will be asleep for quite a while until we get back to the sanctuary, and then we can get him checked out fully," said Jake.

Jake and Jamie then proceeded to carry the tiger back to the coach, followed by Rachel with the medical kit and the trap now disabled/secured, then the crowd of villagers around them started to applaud and cheered them as they walked past.

As for the young man, by now he was calm and started to walk with Jake and Jamie, then he said, "My name is Abdul, and these are my people from the village."

Jake then said, "A pleasure to meet you Abdul, my name is Jake, this is Jamie, and the young lady behind us is Rachel, would you like to come back and help us nurse the young tiger?"

Jamie and Rachel then said, "Hello, Abdul."

Finally, back at the coach, they carried the tiger carefully on board snoring, then Jake said, "Vinh, please can you take us to the sanctuary". Lisa, please keep the children and Lady back, the rest of you, we need to watch the tiger to ensure it does now wake up," then he said, "he can only be a year old, and will need all the help we can give it, I pray the tiger will survive, this is an endangered species, such a shame these wonderful animals have to be trapped, suspect this is poachers, will need to inform the authorities when we get back."

Soon they had arrived at the sanctuary, they then disembarked carrying the young tiger to a holding pen specially built for animal casualties. Jake then administered a drug to wake the tiger up, then he said, "Right, all, let's leave the tiger to wake up, we need to watch around the clock, monitoring the tiger's progress, as the next few hours will be critical for the young animal."

Then Abdul said, "May I watch over him?"

Jake then said, "But of course, I will stay with you to see if he is alright," and then all of a sudden the young tiger started to move, at first a bit wobbly on his feet, and not putting pressure on the injured paw.

Then, the young tiger started to lay down near some bushes, trying to lick his paw with the bandage on, then laid his head down on the ground and fell asleep.

Everyone watched eagerly, then Jake said, "Mike, can you please call the local police and report the incident, and ask them to keep a watchful eye out for poachers and trappers in the surrounding area? Also call Max, the Vet, to visit as soon as he can," with that Mike nodded and rushed off to the hut. Then Jake looked at the rest of the party and then said, "now, please, all of you go to the hut, have some food and rest, I will be in later."

Lisa then proceeded to kiss Jake on the cheek, and then said, "He will be OK, won't he?" wiping a tear from her face, the children all by now tired after a long journey, and upset at what they have just seen.

"Lisa, we can only pray, he has a nasty injury, but he is young and I think he will pull through, now you all go to the hut," then he proceeded to give the three children and Lisa a hug, then he said, "Come on, boys, go with Lisa, it's been a long day and we are all tired, for some of us it will be a long night ahead."

The main hut (more of a house than a hut) at the sanctuary was able to accommodate twenty people, the bedrooms were situated on the first floor, with a reasonable size sitting room, large kitchen, with adjoining toilets and showers, and at the back of the hut was a large medical facility, with a room to treat injured animals, an operating theatre with a recovery room. There were two smaller huts with sleeping areas to accommodate another ten people, if need be, with toilet and shower facilities.

That night, the staff all took turns on the night shift to stay and check on the tiger, which was still fast asleep in its pen, by early hours of the morning Richard came running into the main hut were everyone was staying.

Excitement in his voice Richard said, "The young tiger is awake, he tried to wash his paw again, then he got up and started to walk around his pen with a limp," with that news they all rushed out of the hut with excitement and hearts pounding to see the young tiger, hotly pursued by Lady.

"Now, all of you, let's calmly walk towards the pen and not startle the young tiger in his new surroundings," said Jake with a sigh of relief and a happy tone to his voice.

They all stared in amazement at the young tiger, Lady trying to get closer to the Tiger from the pen, inquisitively as usual, but also to make friends.

"Now, Lady, stay back you may get hurt, my love," said Lisa, gently patting her on the head, Lady then looked up at Lisa, with those puppy dog eyes.

Then she said, "Oh, Lady, I know, my love, you want to make friends with him."

The children excited at seeing the tiger alive.

David then turned to his mum, and said, "Why must some people do so much harm to this beautiful animal?" tears started to roll down his face, Lisa could see it was breaking his little heart. Then Lady sensing David's distress began to nuzzle up close to him for comfort. David wrapped his hands around her mane and soaking her mane with his tears.

"David, come, my love, dry your eyes," said Lisa as she then gave him a big hug, and then she said, "unfortunately, not everyone shares your love for these wonderful animals, but also these people do not respect their place on this earth, their only interest is greed and money, sad to say," said Lisa in a soft voice, then Benjamin and Omar went over to hug

David, while Lady was nestled in between them all, and trying to reassure them, a very emotional sight to watch.

Mike then said, "David, it is up to us as conservationists to educate these people to respect these wonderful animals, their habitats, and their role in the world, which we should all love and care for," with a saddened tone to his voice. Then he said, "But, you have to remember also the hard work the local people do to help care, protect and manage these wonderful habitats for the animals that live within, they are the true custodians and guardians," with a smile on his face.

Jake then said, "I agree it is about time the people in this world realised that we must learn to share, care for and act as good custodians/guardians as well, one way is to educate more people and get them involved in wildlife conservation." Then he turned to the team and said, "Jamie, can you please get some meat and let's try and see if we can tempt the young tiger to eat."

Jamie then said, "No problem, Jake," then left with Prashiwa to collect the meat from the fridge.

Then from around the back of the pen, Vinh appeared with a rather sleepy Abdul, and then said, "Well look who I have found fast asleep at the back of the pen," in a soft voice.

Abdul yawning and then wiping his eyes, then said, "I just wanted to stay with the young tiger to ensure he was alright, he means a lot to me and my people, as do all our wildlife," the words spoken just touched everyone's heart.

"See, David, Abdul is one of the caring people in the world, I wish more people would be like him, well done Abdul," said Jake, then patted him on the back, "well done, my friend."

Jamie and Prashiwa then returned with a bucket containing the meat, then they said, "I hope this enough, I do hope the young tiger is hungry," in a caring tone.

"Right, now, everybody, please stand back, while I open the pen door and quickly put the meat into the pen, Rachel and Aarus please can you distract the tiger, while I am doing this," said a cautious Jake.

Rachel and Aarus went to the side of the pen to distract the young tiger's attention with a small piece of meat, which the tiger followed eagerly, they then pushed the meat through the pen bars, which then fell to the floor and the tiger responded by quickly eating the piece of meat.

Then, the tiger started scenting the air with his nose, and moved back to the other side of the pen were there was a quantity of meat placed on the ground.

They all then watched the tiger gingerly move towards the very large chunks of meat, sniffing them, then grabbing one with its paw, and then he moved off to a corner of the pen where he laid down and started to tear at the meat.

"Come now, let's leave the tiger in peace, and have some breakfast ourselves, and that includes you my friend Abdul," said Jake, and then he said, "come on, now, Lady, he is not going to leave you any of his food, your food is in the hut," then chuckling at Lady's facial expression as she sat looking at the tiger eating his meal, then Jake and Abdul started walking back to the hut.

Followed eventually, by Lady, now head up high, wagging her tail from side to side, you could not help but laugh at her, what a character.

Then rest of the party then followed, back to the hut, to sit down and tuck into a light breakfast consisting of cornflakes with ice cold milk from the fridge, a plate of hot buttered toast, a selection of fresh fruit including bananas, mangos, lychees, papayas, coconuts, peaches, pears and kiwis, various fruit juices and mugs of refreshing tea.

Lady, on the other hand, laid down tucking into a bowl of cooked meat and biscuits which she heartily cleared within minutes, then she got up and started to drink from her water bowl, the refreshing cold water, then she finally went to her bed and laid down.

While they were all eating, they listened to a selection of music being played on the radio, including 'Born Free', 'Everlasting Love', 'Band of Gold', Electro Velvet 'Still In Love With You', and 'I Can't Help Myself', the words to these songs did catch them all with joy and emotion in their hearts. Especially, Jake with the song 'Born Free' being played, who then tried brushing a tear from his eye, without trying to catch anyone's attention.

Then, after a short while, there was a sound of a van and then it appeared, Lady's ears pricked up and then she got up and walked towards the front door. Jake then got up from his chair, and looked at the window, and said, "It is OK, it's Max, the vet, now all of you finish your breakfast, while I see Max," then he turned and said, "Abdul would you like to come with me?"

Abdul nodded with excitement in his eyes, then Jake said, "Now, Lady, you stay here, while we check the young Tiger with Max."

Lady sat with ears back, and butter-would-not-melt-eyes that would truly melt anyone's heart, Jake then stroked her on the head, smiled, and then left with Abdul.

"Hi, Max, I see you and your assistant have spotted the new patient," said Jake.

"Well, Jake, what a handsome young tiger, he certainly is not old enough to leave his mother yet, so I wonder what has happened, anyway the important thing is to check the young tiger's paw," said Max, as Max then proceeded to load the injection into the gun. While his assistant Karl, and Abdul tried to draw the young tiger's attention to them, with that Max aimed and fired the gun, the injection hit the rump of the tiger, who then fell to the ground.

"Right let us proceed into the pen, the tranquiliser has started to work, the tiger will be out for a while, enough time for me to check the injured paw," said Max.

Watch from a short distance was Lisa, the children, the conservation team, the Sherpas, and Lady on her lead.

Max then proceeded to unwrapped the dressing, and then checked the paw thoroughly, he then turned and said, "Well a very lucky young tiger, he has a very strong paw, and the trap was not strong enough to do much harm, anyway, I will give him some antibiotics and pain reliever," as he proceeded to put on a new dressing on the paw.

Then he said, "Right, I will now give the young tiger another injection to wake him up, so I suggest you all leave the pen now, and I then will follow," Max left the pen, and then Jake safely secured the pen door behind him.

They all watched patiently as the tiger started to wake up, a bit wobbly on his feet at first, then he slowly moved towards the bushes to lay down.

"Well, Jake, I will pop back tomorrow to check on him again, just keep an eye on him for now, he will recover in good time and will be able to walk on his paw again, for now, peace and quiet is what he needs," said Max.

Then he said, "I will contact the local villagers and the police authorities about the poachers and their traps, any found to be destroyed, but more importantly try to see if we can find this young tiger's mother, if possible, and, Jake, we must all do our bit to put an end to the poaching of the wildlife."

Jake then said, "I totally agree with you, thank you, Max, for all your help, and we will see you tomorrow," at that point Abdul sat next to the pen watching the young tiger in his charge.

Lady then barked.

"I see you have a new addition to the team, what is her name?" said Max as he headed back to the van with his assistant Karl, and turned waving back to them all.

Jake, then said, "Yes, this is Lady, she is part of the conservation project."

The van then started to leave the sanctuary, as the people waved goodbye.

Then, all of a sudden, a police car appeared in the drive, Jake stepped forwarded followed by Richard with the trap and handed it to the sergeant as evidence.

Sergeant Lin then got out of the car and approached Jake and Richard, then said, "Thank you for the call, I see the injured patient in the pen. People, when will they learn to share this world with our fellow animals, and stop killing them?" he paused then said, "I have some good news, Jake, first of all no more animals have been trapped, and I had a call later yesterday from a village nearby, a man ended up caught in his own trap, he is now in police custody and awaiting trial, the local judge is a keen conservationist, so a harsh sentence will be imposed with a large fine, he will be in prison for many years, he has also confessed who his partners involved in the poaching are, so they are being apprehended, and will suffer the same fate."

"That is great news Sergeant, any news of the young tiger's mother?" said Jake.

"Funny you should say that, one of the local villagers has heard a tiger call, it could be his mother. I do hope so, and one day they can both be reunited again," said Sergeant Lin, smiling.

He then finally said, "Well, must dash, doing a talk at a local school on law and order, you must join and do a talk on wildlife conservation, the kids would love it. Oh, and this beauty, is your new recruit, Lady, I believe? Local people have been talking about her."

With that, Lady barked in recognition, and tilting her head as she catches the words spoken.

"Yes, this is young Lady," said Jake with a smile.

Then Sergeant Lin returned to the police car, waving goodbye to everyone, and then the car drove off.

Richard then turned to Jake and said, "Do you really think that could be the call of the young tiger's mother? As we do hear the odd male tiger calling at times, it would be great if it was," with a glint in his eyes of excitement, and wishing it to be true.

"Do hope so, Richard, it would be wonderful to feel that we can reunite the young tiger with his mother," said Jake.

With that Abdul looked at them both, and then said, "It is only a matter of time, she will appear to be with the young male, and it is a mother's natural instinct to find her lost offspring."

Over time the sanctuary staff, if they were not caring for the other animals in the sanctuary, were undertaking the night and day patrols with the dogs looking for any poachers and destroying any traps they come across.

They were busy mending the perimeter fencing around the wildlife park, or planting in areas of the forest, partly destroyed by fire over grazing or landslides, or teaching the villagers and the local school children on how to care for their wildlife and the amazing habitats.

But they would also come and spend time watching the young tiger, he like many other animals are so endangered and so precious, they deserved their help, (song 'Run' by Leona Lewis).

To see the young tiger starting to recover well and gaining his strength, but also to see him able to walk on his injured paw without any discomfort, and noticing that the wound, which had now healed well. They all felt for the young tiger so much for what he had gone through, you can't help but love him. Sometimes, Jake would sit with Abdul in the evenings watching the young tiger, tears rolling down Jakes face, he truly felt for his young charge.

This did catch Lisa watching from a distance, she could see Jake was so emotionally charged, the pain he showed at times, but seeing the other side of him, he was so passionate and cared so much for those animals in his care, she was so proud to be with him, but also the love he had for the Nepalese people and other races he met overtime.

Lisa thought after losing David, the love of her life, that she would never find another person, but fortune had casted its net out and now Jake had appeared in her, and her young son's life, and yes, even Lady's.

But also, David and Lady were settling down with their new surroundings, new friends, seeing the wonderful wildlife and their habitats. They were also developing and forming a strong bond especially with Jake, Omar and Benjamin.

Then one day Benjamin, David and Omar walked over to Lisa and David and said, "We would like to call the young tiger Shikari (the hunter)" (and what a name for such an impressive animal), David with the glint in his eyes, and that smile.

Lisa and Jake then together said, "What a wonderful name for a beautiful and majestic animal,"

Then Jake said, "Now please do not get too attached, as one day Shikari will have to be released back into the wild, which is his home, but for now let us all enjoy every moment with him, he will love this attention."

Lisa then smiled, and then said, "I am so proud of you boys, the love you show to Shikari, and the other wild animals is so amazing, and as for you, Lady, the motherly instinct you show for Shikari is so wonderful, brings a tear to my eye," with that Lady tilted her head and then barked with appreciation for the praise given.

At times the children would just love sitting and watching Shikari move around the enclosure with such majestic stature, brushing his head against the tree branches, also now and then he would scent mark his territory.

Other times Shikari would roll over onto his back rubbing against the ground from side to side, and then he would proceed to start grooming himself, licking himself all over, and then moving towards the bars on the enclosure and start brushing his head up and down, you could see that he was totally enjoying himself, this certainly amused the children who would sit and watch with interest for hours, while Lady would sit, watching the young tiger, tilting her head from side to side, he fascinated her so much.

One bit the children were totally fascinated with, was when it was feeding time, part of an animal carcase would be put into the enclosure, the young tiger would start to crouch on all fours, tail wagging side to side, and then with great force he would pounce on the carcase, and then proceed to tear the flesh into manageable pieces, ready to devour, this made the children giggle and laugh, Shikari would look at them and then would continue enjoying tucking into his meal.

Poor Lady would sitting tilting her head side to side, then yelping thinking that a piece of meat would come her way, on one occasion Lisa noticed this reaction, and said in a gentle tone, "Come, Lady, let Shikari enjoy his meal in peace, I have a nice bowl of cooked meat and biscuits waiting for you inside, my love."

With that Lady got up, wagging her tail, brushing head against Lisa as they started to walk back towards the hut, ready to tuck into her dinner, you just have to smile at her.

There were, however, times that they noticed on several occasions that Shikari would be calling, they would watch from a safe distance to see what may happen, but they never saw nothing, this did puzzle them, and they would wonder who he was trying to attract attention to. Jake and the team did wonder if Shikari was trying to see if his mother was about, these were very emotional times for all of them.

Then, one day a couple of the Sherpas noticed Shikari calling in the early morning, maybe his mother was nearby and thought the logical explanation was that he was calling for his mother, as after all he was a young tiger and would still be dependent on his mother in the wild.

Jake did ponder, and thought this was after all what the young tiger was hoping for, to be with his mother, which is after all a natural instinct for a young animal to be with its parents and siblings for comfort, security, and reassurance.

So, then the day finally came after much thought, discussion and preparation by the conservation team, it was now time for the young tiger to be released back into the wild, a very emotional time for all of them, the children especially were in tears, but they all knew this was the kindest thing to do, Shikari was, after all, a wild animal and he deserved to be given that chance to be released back into the wild, were he truly belongs, then playing on the radio was 'Wish Upon A Star ', which they all joined in and started to sing, with joy in their hearts, while outside there was a heavy downpour of rain.

That morning during breakfast, which was indeed a very solemn occasion for all, especially for the children, Jake and Richard said to the children in a gentle voice, "This was Shikari's time, to be able to be released back into his own surroundings, were he would find comfort and the security of the forest again."

Then Lisa said, "Now, come on children, wipe those tears from your little faces, it is sad for all of us, but Shikari has been given the chance to go back into the wild, some animals never do, let's all be happy for him, and put those happy faces on."

Then Lisa turned the radio on, the song that started playing by popular request, was 'I Can't Help Myself' sung by The Four Tops, then 'Everlasting Love', and then followed by '(Your Love Keeps Lifting Me) Higher And Higher', she was trying to lift everyone's spirits up, on this sad occasion.

Then, after breakfast had finished, they all then went over to the enclosure were Shikari was by now pacing up and down, in his own way he knew something was going to happen.

Jake then said, "Now, please keep your distance, while we proceed to dart Shikari."

Finally, Shikari was then sedated from a dart, he then moved over to one side of his enclosure and then laid down, after a short while, Jake and two of the Sherpas then proceeded with extreme caution and safety into his enclosure, then Jake proceeded to check over Shikari to ensure he was asleep and to remove the dart.

Then Jake with the help of the two Sherpas gently placed Shikari onto a stretcher, and proceeded to carry him out of the enclosure, then Jamie and Mike helped them to put Shikari safely into his crate, situated at the back of the open truck, the children all watching with awe.

Finally, they all proceeded to climb into the truck, the children followed in a jeep with Lisa and one of the Sherpas driving.

Driving a short distance along the road they noticed on the way that the heavy rain last night, had left its mark, with deep pools of water, the air was humid, some trees along the way had come down, with nearby villagers helping to clear them from the roadsides, we all waved at them as we passed them by.

After a while, they finally arrived at the edge of the mountain forest reserve, then they parked the vehicles up near a small clearing.

Jake then climbed out of the truck to check on Shikari in his crate, followed by Jamie, Richard and Mike and the Sherpas.

Lisa, the children, and of course, Lady stayed within the jeep, but had a good view of the truck with the crate on, waiting eagerly for the release of Shikari.

Jake and his team, found Shikari still asleep, then Jake beckoned the team to help lift the crate onto the ground away from the truck and the jeep, to be placed in a position where Lisa and the children could watch in safety with the release of Shikari.

Then Jake opened the crate door, by now Shikari was starting to come around, then they all started to move back away from the crate, watching with anticipation, when Shikari would leave the crate.

Finally, Shikari got up, and left his crate, wobbling slightly on his feet for the first few seconds, then composing himself. He turned, looked at us all, roared, then started calling several times, then he ran towards the forest edge, only to be greeted by an adult female tiger and a young tiger by her side. We then realised, knowing in own hearts, that Shikari all the time was actually calling for his mother, what a beautiful reunion. Shikari was rubbing up to his mother and his sibling, and then tears of joy started rolling down their faces, they all then started to hug each other, so emotionally, but so proud of what they had experienced, wishing Shikari a happy life now with his family.

Then Shikari looked at them for the last time, and then followed his mother and his sibling back into the safety of the forest canopy.

Omar then said, "How did Shikari's mother know, where he was?"

Jake said, "Well, Omar, she always knew, she had been visiting regularly at his enclosure for some time, also he was calling now and then to her, this is quite natural, a tiger cub normally stays with his mother for about two to three years before he makes his own way in the world beyond."

Then Jake paused, to notice the sad expression on Omar's face, then he further said, "Omar, the mother was never going to give up, so that is why she followed us to the rescue site, they were waiting for his eventual release, it is a mother's instinct to be with her cub, a bond that is so strong between a mother and her cubs."

Then he said, "Like there is a strong bond between you, me, and Benjamin, an eternal bond, you both mean so much to me, and I do love you both so dearly."

"Likewise, the same applies to the mother tiger and her cubs, especially the reuniting of her cub Shikari," he further said, and then Jake proceeded to give Omar a big hug.

Then with that, they all climbed into the vehicles, this time Jake drove the jeep with Lisa, the children, and Richard, while the rest of the team were in the truck, with some of the Sherpas and Mike at the back watching over the crate.

While in the jeep, Lisa then said, "Shall we have some music to try and cheer us up?" as she turned the radio on, it was the Four Tops singing cheerful melodies, 'If I Were A Carpenter', followed by 'Bernadette', 'Walk Away Renee', 'Simple Game', 'Rooms Of Gloom', and then 'I Can't Help Myself', while they were driving along the road.

After a short while, they were then suddenly stopped by a couple of very distraught male villagers, who were anxiously trying to flag them down.

Jake pulled up, and opened the door, got out and approached the villagers with one of the Sherpas, though Jake could speak a reasonable amount of Nepalese, Vinh, his lead Sherpa, could speak fluent Nepalese, which was one of a number of languages he was fluent in, and therefore could help Jake with the conversation with the villagers.

Then Jake with Vinh greeted the two men, and then said, "Please, my friends, what has happened, why are you both so distraught?"

One of the men named Aakash then said, "Please help us, our village nearby was struck by a landslide, some of our people are trapped inside their houses." He then said, "They all had been working hard to free their people, but needed more help," in a very distraught tone to his voice.

Then Jake said, "Please can you show us the way, and we will help you to free your people, my friend?"

Jake then left with Aakash walking towards the jeep, while Vinh and Aakash's friend called Temuji headed off towards the truck, still very shaken up.

Before driving off, Jake then got onto the radio asking for further medical assistance from his colleagues back at the conservation centre, and to also ask for help from the villages nearby.

They then drove off, heading up towards a very narrow track towards what they could see was what was left of the village, some trees and mud from the landslide had damaged a few houses near the hillside, while the villagers were eagerly trying to clear the debris as best they could.

The two vehicles were parked up near the road, then they all left the jeep and truck heading towards the villagers, eagerly to help where they could.

Jake and the team got to work helping the village -men-folk remove the debris from the damaged houses, to make a clear path, so that they could gain access inside without causing the foundations to fall in, especially the rooftops, while doing this they could hear calling, they then stopped, and listened to hear if there were any sounds from within the building.

While Lisa and the children helped to tend to the wounds of the injured villagers, bathing and then dressing their wounds as best they could. In a nearby house, now converted into a makeshift hospital, some of the women villagers were heating up by the fireside, a type of hot tea to give to the injured.

While this was going on, Jamie noticed Lady running towards a house nearby, which was badly damaged by a fallen tree that had caused part of the roof to cave in, Lady started scratching and making a commotion trying to make her way in, she could hear the sounds of a couple of people, calling from within.

Jamie then turned and shouted for some help, Vinh and Aahask acknowledged him and then raced towards Jamie who was by now trying to remove the building debris and then calling to the people inside, by now he could also hear the sounds of a baby's cry.

Lady by now was inside, and by the side of the man and woman huddled in the corner and clutching a little baby in their arms, unfortunately next to them lay a little boy still and motionless. Lady moved towards the boy and licked him, trying to keep him warm.

Finally Jamie, Vinh, and Aahask managed to make their way in, careful not to cause the fragile timbers holding onto what was left of the roof to fall, slowly and carefully the little boy was carried out followed by his mother and baby, and then the father.

They then made their way towards the house where the injured were being cared for.

Jamie carrying the little boy, wrapped up in a blanket, with Lady by his side.

Lisa noticing the new arrivals, then rushed over to Jamie, and then said, "please lay the little boy down here," she then felt for a pulse. Thankfully, he was alive, but knocked out, gently checking for any bruising around the head, strangely there was nothing, then all of a sudden Lady moved closer to the little boy, picking up that he was about to go into a fit. This puzzled Lisa a bit.

The boy then started to go straight into a fit, Lady staying by the boy's side closely, the mother with the baby nearby watching, the father trying also to comfort his son, Lisa turned to Jamie, and then said, "I am not sure for certain, but this little boy suffers from fits, he probably has some form of epilepsy, we must comfort him until he finally comes around, he will need urgent medical assistance."

Finally the boy did come around, dazed and very unsure of himself, Lady remaining constantly by his side for reassurance, a very touching sight for all to watch.

The boy's father, brushing the hair on the little boy's head, with tears rolling down his face, then he said in Nepalese, "My little ray of sunshine, my Nesar," then proceeded to cuddle his son, by now the mother and baby were next to them as well, reassuring each other.

Jamie then turned to Lisa and said, "But, how did Lady know that the little boy would be going into a fit, It's truly amazing."

Lisa then said, "It has been a known fact that animals, in particular dogs, can sense when a person is going into a fit, it is just amazing, but there are many animals that will help other animals and even humans when there is some form of danger," then she proceeded to stroke Lady on the head, and then said, "you clever girl."

Then, finally, a doctor arrived and came straight over to where the little boy was laying down, the doctor then introduced himself, and said, "My name is Tao," then said, "how is this little boy doing?"

Lisa then said, "This little boy, called Nesar, has had what I think is an epileptic fit, thankfully my dog Lady picked up the symptoms before we knew it."

Doctor Tao then said, "Yes that is true, dogs are very good at detecting the start of a fit, and will stay close to that person Nature is such a wonderful thing. But, I think for now, this little boy will need to go to hospital for treatment for his epilepsy, with some of the other seriously injured patients that would need further treatment and stay overnight in the hospital."

Then the boy's father turned and said to us all, "thank you," then he gently proceeded to carry his son Nesar out of the house, then headed towards. The two hospital vans were parked next to the jeep, while Doctor Tao proceeded to check the new patients that had just been brought in with various injures, thankfully, many of the patients had just sustained shock, minor cuts and bruises, so they were treated there and then.

It was going to be a long night for Lisa, and the team, tending to the injured in the makeshift hospital overseen by Doctor Tao and a couple of his nurses, helping the villagers as best they could, while some of the rescuers, including a couple of Ghurkhas and the Sherpas from the conservation centre, had started to set up makeshift huts to house some of the now homeless villagers, also providing them with warm drinks, food and blankets to keep them warm.

But this was not the end, later that night Lady had disappeared, up the hill, followed by Jake, Mike and one of the Sherpas with torches in hot pursuit. Lady had heard the sounds of animals crying coming from a small cave up above.

Finally, Jake, Mike and a Sherpa arrived at the edge of the cave to find two small snow leopard cubs huddled together near their dead mother, Lady sitting nearby.

This truly puzzled Jake, especially as the mother snow leopard seemed healthy at first, then on further inspection he noticed a small residue of foam from the side of the mother's mouth, the body was still warm and rigor mortis had not set in yet, he then said in a sad tone to his voice, " I think she may been poisoned, but not sure, something does not seem right, having said this, it is very upsetting for all of us to see, but more so distressing for her cubs who have lost their mother," and then he proceeded to check the two cubs over, from what he could see on inspection, they seemed OK, so far, but further tests would need to be carried out on them.

Then he said anxiously, "We must hurry and get the cubs back to the village so that I can undertake a full examination on these cubs and especially the mother, hopefully I pray they have not ingested any of the foam or suckled from their mother's teats."

So they wrapped up the cubs as best they could to keep them warm, while the Sherpa carried the mother's body, tears welling up in all of their eyes, such an emotional sight that touched their hearts and very souls, they proceeded down the hill with Lady by their side.

On the way down, Mike spotted them then said, "This is terrible, who could have done this? We have educated all the villagers not to use any poison on any of the wildlife, now this has happened, what a tragedy," in a sad tone to his voice.

Jake then said, "I can only assume one of the farmers chose not to follow our advice, knowing that it is illegal to poison any of the wildlife, we all know that leopards will take cattle as they are easy prey, but I thought the regular talks we have had with the local farmers and villagers, on how to protect their cattle, and goats during the day and also by keeping them securely locked in the barns for the night, and watched over by a shepherd would have helped."

He then said further, "The use of poison is totally illegal, especially on all wildlife, and is protected by law, of course policing is another issue, this is a reasonable size country, with a lot of land to cover, so education to its people is crucial."

Then finally he said, "Tomorrow we must investigate who is using poisons if it is anyone? However, we must instil into the villagers the terrible harm that can be done to the wild animals if poisons are used, causing them unnecessary suffering, and the harm if accidentally taken by any of their domesticated animals, and even more so, if ingested by an adult or even a child. This is so serious."

Mike then said, "For now we must check these cubs over for any side effects, I do pray that they have not ingested any of the poison, if it is a poison. God I do pray, it breaks my hearts if the results are positive, that we have to put these two cubs to sleep."

Finally they arrived at the village, Lisa spotted them and raced over, then said, "Oh my God, what has happened?"

Jake then said, "Thanks to Lady, we hopefully may have come in time to save the two cubs, fingers crossed, but unfortunately it is too later for their mother, we need to get to our tent."

As they entered the tent, Jake asked the Sherpa to place the mother on the table ready for examination, while he and Mike then undertook a full examination of the cubs, who by now were so frightened and fearful, taking only a tiny amount of blood and saliva samples, then they waited eagerly for the results of the tests, they thankfully all came back negative, which then puzzled Jake, wondering how the mother had finally met her death, and the cause of the death."

Vinh and Richard then entered in the tent, Richard said, "just heard, what a tragedy, what can we do to help?"

Vinh then said, "We must get some fluid into the cubs or they will not last the night, they are so small," so Vinh proceeded to start to feed the young cubs one after the other, from a bottle with a teat on the end, ready for them to start suckling onto, which they accepted willingly in turn, then once their little bellies were full, he then wrapped them up in a warm blanket to keep them warm, and placed them in a cage, guarded over by Lady.

Lisa then said, "Well it seems, we may have a surrogate mother for the little cubs," wiping a tear from her face.

Jake then said, "Yes, it looks like she is going to be their surrogate mother, but the cubs are still not over the worst, tomorrow will tell if they have survived the night, I will watch over them tonight, Richard if you can take over in the morning, for me, please."

"No problem Jake," said Richard.

Jake then said, "Lisa, how are the children, and the villagers now?" in a concerned tone to his voice.

Lisa then said, "The children are fast asleep with some of the village children in a makeshift hut, the seriously injured villagers have all been taken to the hospital now, and the rest of the villagers are trying to settle down for the night in makeshift accommodation."

Lisa then said further, "Sadly a few of the villagers have been found dead in a couple of the houses, including a family with two little children, Jake, it is so tragic," tears by now rolling down her face.

She then said, "The bodies have been placed in a tent ready to be buried tomorrow."

"I know it has been a very sad day for all of us, but we must help the living, but never forget those that have died, they will always be remembered in our hearts," said a very solemn Jake, while cuddling Lisa in his arms, then he said "there, there, my love," in a soft and gentle reassuring tone to his voice, then kissed her on the forehead.

Then Lisa kissed Jake on the cheek and said, "Yes, a very sad day indeed, Jake, after saying goodbye to Shikari the young tiger, then this terrible tragedy, such a loss of life, it breaks my heart."

"I know it is so terrible, my love, but we must carry on and help those that need our help now," said Jake.

Lisa then said, "Good night, Jake, you are such an inspiration to us all," and then headed off to check on the children in the nearby house, and also the injured people in the makeshift hospital.

Then Jake went over to the table and proceeded to exam the mother leopard, the expression on his face said it all, while examining the body. Lady as usual looked on at Jake, her ear pricked back, with the sad expression on her face, while also watching over her two new charges.

(Then music from a nearby radio, was then playing, "Love Never Dies")

Richard, Jamie and Mike looked on, while Jake carefully examined the body, their emotions were so high, tears rolling down all of their faces.

Then Jake trying to compose himself, wiping his face, he then said, "I am at a loss for what has caused her death, even more so, the foaming around her mouth."

Then all of a sudden, Max the local vet appeared in the tent, and said, "Heard the terrible news and rushed over here, Jake, you are shaking, here, let me exam the female snow leopard."

The rest just looked on, while Max thoroughly checked over the body, then undertook further tests, and then he went over to carefully check the two cubs, watched over by Lady.

"Well, Lady, your motherly instincts have kicked in, you are doing a great job on looking after your charges" said Max, then gently placed them one by one next to Lady, who then proceeded to lick them, and then the cubs started to nuzzle up to Lady again her body for warmth.

"Hmm," said Max rather puzzled at first, the expression on his face.

Then he said, "Well that definitely rules out that she has been poisoned, I think from closer examination she has had stroke or seizure, but what caused this to happen, possibly stress of some sort," he then paused and then said, "my friends, the trouble is, there is not that much research done of the lives of the snow leopards, apart from being very rare, they are extremely illusive animals, and living in very isolated and dangerous places, many inaccessible by man". Then he said further, "I will stay here for the night to help with the nursing of the two cubs, and then early tomorrow morning, if one of you could show me where you found her."

Jake said, "That is great news to hear, Max, especially for the two cubs, but so sad for their mother, I hope she died quickly the thought is terrible and must have been distressing for the two cubs to see." Then he said, "I will go with you early tomorrow morning to the cave where we found her."

Jake then said, "Now, Max and myself will stay here to watch over the leopard cubs, with Lady, now all of you try and have a good night's sleep and thank you, my friends, for what you all have done today."

The rest of night came and went for Jake and Max, watching over the cubs, with Lady by their side, by now both of them were terribly exhausted, then Richard finally arrived in the early hours of the morning to take over for Jake and Max.

Jake, then said, in a joyous tone to his voice, "Morning, Richard, well the cubs have come through, two extremely lucky little cubs, and they have had another good feed, Lady as usual, acting as a great surrogate mother to them both," by now Jake was yawning, and ready for bed.

"Now go on, Jake and Max, try and have a few hours' sleep both of you, we have a very busy day ahead of us," said Richard, in a soft voice so as not to disturb the two cubs curled up together with Lady who were all fast asleep on a large blanket, but with joy in his face because the cubs had survived the night.

Then all of a sudden Richard looked underneath the table said softly, "I see we are not alone."

"Yes, it is Abdul, he came in after you all left last night, to help watch the snow leopard cubs, but so shattered fell asleep early this morning, so we put a spare blanket over him, and he has been there ever since, we will let him be, to sleep on," said Jake.

"Well I don't know about you, Jake, but I am ready for a few hours' sleep," said Max, stretching his arms and yawning, then left the tent.

"Right, Richard, I am off now, Lady will stay with you, she has just been brilliant, if you could have just seen her last night as the two cubs laid next to her for comfort, she started to wash them, it was such a touching sight to see, Lady is just a natural. Any problems, let Max and me know, but I think we are over the worse now," said Jake, with an emotional tone to his voice, but also in his heart so proud of Lady.

Then finally, Jake stroked Lady on the head, and said, "Thank you, my love, you are an amazing dog and what a great mother you will make," then he got up and then said, "I will see you later on, Richard." Then finally, Jake left the tent, heading off towards the house where Lisa, Max and the children were staying.

Yawning as he walked along, ready to go to bed for a few hours and for a well-deserved sleep, he was completely exhausted and tired, it had been a very eventful previous day, full of sadness, especially the loss of human lives and of the female snow leopard, but not also forgetting Shikari the young tiger, wiping a tear from his face as he walked into the house, trying now to disturb the people inside fast asleep. Then he finally laid down and fell fast asleep next to Lisa and the three boys.

The following morning after they all had a wash, got dressed, followed by a light breakfast, Lisa, the boys, the village children with some of the mothers, then continued with their daily chores.

Jake and Max went back to the tent where the leopards were being cared for. Jake then said, "Richard, how are the two cubs doing?" as he watched them fast asleep and cuddled up to Lady.

Then all of a sudden the blanket moved and Abdul appeared, stretching his arms, and looking sheepish at them all, "Well good morning Abdul, now, pop over to the house where Lisa is and have some breakfast, and we will see you later on," said Jake with a smile on his face, patting Abdul on the back, and then said, "thank you, my friend," as Abdul then left the tent.

Richard then said, "The cubs are doing well and have been fed, and as you can see they are fast asleep," Lady on the other hand was awake by now, then having a good stretch before laying back down next to the cubs.

Max then said, "Well the young cubs seem to be looking OK to me, so rather than disturb them for now, I will check on them later, but for now, Jake, if you can show me where you found the mother and cubs?"

"Right, Richard, we will see you later on, and, Max, please follow me," said Jake.

Then they set off towards the place where the mother and two cubs were found in a cave up above.

Meanwhile, back at the village, one of the Sherpas with Mike came in to take over for Richard to watch over the cubs and Lady. Richard then thanked Mike and the Sherpa, then he headed off to have some breakfast.

Back at the cave, Max then checked the cave for any signs that could have triggered the female snow leopard's death, while Jake stood and watched a forensic detective at work.

"Well, Jake, clearly there is nothing I can see here that could have caused her death, the only obvious possibility is the landslide, which could have somehow triggered her death. It's a known fact that when there is immediate danger the mother will protect her young from any harm, a sad fact and an even more so, a tragic loss," said Max.

"And I thought she may have possibly been poisoned," said Jake.

"An easy assumption, my friend, to make, but thankfully for the two cubs it was not or they would have been dead as well. Chin up, Jake, you now have two new charges to look after, and I am going to enjoy studying these illusive and majestic animals," said Max.

"Well, a challenge for us all, but a nice one, the years I have been living here, I have only heard the stories from the villagers living high up in the mountains about the snow leopards, but I have never seen one, until last night," said Jake.

Then he said, "Well, we better make our way back down towards the village."

Finally Jake and Max arrived back at the village to be joined by Lisa, the boys and the conservation team, ready to attend the sky burial ritual.

But before that, Jake and Max popped into the tent to check on Lady and the two cubs, now being watched over by Abdul and one of the Sherpas from another village called Lushant.

But before they left the tent, Jake then turned and said, "Now, Lady, look after your two babies, I am so proud of you, my darling girl."

Lady then looked up, tilting her head, that expression on her face just melted his heart, while the little cubs then stretched and then snuggled back up to Lady's body.

"Now, Abdul and Lushant, the bottles of milk are on the table, when the cubs wake up for their next feed, next to the bowl of food and water for Lady, we will be back as soon as we can," he then paused and then said, "there will be someone to collect the female snow leopard's body for the sky burial ritual."

Then as Max and Jake, left the tent, they passed a very sad young village Sherpa, heading towards the tent, to collect the mother leopard's body.

Then Lisa, Jake, the three boys, Max with the conservation team followed the villagers and the two Gurkhas. Some of the villagers were carrying the dead bodies of their families and friends, while the young Sherpa was carrying the snow leopard's body, and up front were the Buddhist monks all moving towards the sky burial site up in the mountain, in an orderly procession. Silence was observed by all at the funeral procession, as we all proceeded up towards the mountain, where there was a platform at the top where the bodies would be finally laid to rest.

After half an hour of walking up the narrow pathways, passing rows of colourful prayer flags as we walked along, heading upwards towards the burial site, we had finally arrived.

All that could be heard now were the calls of the vultures and eagles as they circled high up in the skies above (dedicated song, Pie Jesu).

The villagers, carrying the bodies, then proceeded to gently lay the dead bodies on to the platform, then came the young Sherpa who then stepped forward placing the body of the female snow leopard, between the two dead children's bodies, then gently with such passion, he placed their little arms around the snow leopard's body.

Then, all of a sudden, the clouds above broke, as rays of light from the sun shone down onto the bodies on the platform.

Then, as the young Sherpa (who we eventually later knew was called Mansou), stepped back, tears were now rolling down his face, and shaking with grief through his body.

The sight of seeing this emotional scene, caught us all with such emotion and such grief, especially Lisa, Jake, the children, Max, the wildlife team, the Gurkhas, and villagers, many by now wiping the tears from their faces, the grief shown on their faces would touch anyone's heart and soul.

Mansou was so upset over the loss of the female snow leopard, but what we found out later was that the young family that had died were his parents, young brother and sister.

Vinh, then stepped forward to embrace Mansou, who was by now sobbing his heart out into the arms of Vinh, who embraced him like a father does to his son, for Vinh was in fact his cousin.

Vinh then said in a soft voice, "I know, Mansou, it is breaking my heart too, they are now at peace, a wonderful gesture was to place the snow leopard body between your sister Rae Soo, and your brother Genghis, knowing that their souls will rise above to the celestial heaven," as he then placed a kiss on the top of the head of Mansou, and then said, "there, there, my cousin, may they be at peace."

Then Vinh said, "It would be an honour for you to come and live with me and my family, we are your family now."

Mansou then said, as he wiped the tears from his face, "I would be proud to live with you all, but I will need to collect whatever processions left from my home after the ceremony."

"But of course, and I will gladly help you, Mansou," said an emotional Vinh.

Then the next thing that happened was that the senior Buddhist monk stepped forward to recite the words to the sky burial ritual, which touched us all.

Next a couple of Buddhist monks with some of the male villagers stepped forward, and headed towards the platform to partly open the clothes of the dead villagers, partly exposing their bodies ready for the vultures and the birds of prey to feed on.

Sad as it may have been, in particular to us, non-natives, to the Nepalese, and other mountain people, it is said that this act has a significant religious meaning, to allow the dead bodies' souls to rise up into the celestial heavens above, (Krassimir Avramov song 'Illusion').

Then the funeral procession stood still, as a mark of respect of the dead for a while, while the calls of the vultures and eagles finally arrived, circling high up in the skies above, by now in big numbers.

Then the funeral procession started to leave the platform, heading down the pathway towards the village, far below the mountain.

Lisa then trying to console a very tearful David, wiping the tears from his face, the little boy had witnessed a very sad sight, the last time, was at his father's funeral back home.

Meanwhile, Jake put his arms around his two boys, Ben and Omar, both trying to wipe the tears from their faces, then he said, "Now, children, it is such a sad day for us all, but the dead villagers and the snow leopard are now at peace, their souls are now in heaven, and we should all be proud that we have been able to celebrate this solemn occasion, with such dignity and grace, more so, as a lasting sign of respect to them," in a gently tone to his voice, trying to hold back his emotions and tears now welling up around his eyes. Lisa could see it was hurting Jake and put her arm around him to reassure him, underneath, Lisa was falling in love with Jake.

Then he started to compose himself again and then said, "When we get back to the village, shall we all call in and see how Lady is coping with her new charges, the two baby snow leopard cubs, I am sure they would like to see you all?" spoken with such love and affection, and from the heart.

Lisa then said, "Jake, you certainly know how to lift the spirits of the children, after attending such a sad and solemn occasion, I so do love you for saying that," as she then grasped Jake by the hand.

Meanwhile, David joined Omar and Ben, in front of them, by now all excited as they were going to see Lady with the two young snow leopards cubs, the glint in their eyes, and the giggling from them made Lisa and Jake smile.

Finally, they all arrived at the village, astounded by seeing a number of people from other villages, the local police, and the support of an attachment of Gurkhas from the nearby barracks, helping to start rebuilding the houses, it touched their hearts, with a warm glow inside, the funeral party now arriving back at their village, words could not express their feelings for what they saw.

Especially the amazing Gurkha army, as with many of the great armies across the world, for example, the soldiers from Australasia, Asia/Orient, Africa, the Americas, Europe to say but a few, the Gurkhas have always been there to support their fellow nations, through thick and thin, especially during the world wars, we must never forget what they all did, a fitting tribute to them all, and not forgetting the unsung heroes, the animal comrades.

The children were all excited, then Lisa said, "Now, boys, we must be quiet as church mice, when entering the tent, as the cubs may be asleep with Lady.

So, quietly they all entered the tent, a wow factor, the expression on the boys faces said it all. Lady laying there nursing the two cubs, watched on by Abdul, Lushant, and now the young Sherpa called Ajay who then said in a quiet tone to his voice, "Both cubs woke up a while ago and have had another feed, and now are fast asleep as you can all see, cuddled up to Lady."

Jake then said, "That is very good news," then he said, "Has Lady been able to get up and have something to eat at all?"

Abdul then said, "Yes, much to the crying of the snow leopard cubs, but she was able to leave them to go outside for a short while, and then she came back into the tent, then she laid down by them, and started to wash them, before they went back to sleep."

Then the children said, in a quiet tone, "When will we be able to pick them up? They are so sweet and we just want to cuddle them."

Jake then said, "We'll give them a few more days to settle down, then you all will be able to hold them, but remember children these are wild animals, one day they will need to be released back into the wild, therefore they must have minimum human contact."

Then Lushant said, "While watching the cubs feed, I noticed one of the cubs had blue eyes and the other had amber eyes, so beautiful to see, OH, we are so lucky and privileged to be with such majestic animals," spoken with such love and affection.

David, then said, "Cannot wait to see the young cubs open their eyes, and see them start to play, they are so cute, Mum," excitedly.

"Now, David, yes they are cute and cuddly for now, but when they grow up they are different, as Jake has said, they after all wild animals, and we must respect this," said Lisa, as she winked at David.

Then the three children turned to Jake and Lisa and said in a soft tone, "When we grow up we want to be protectors of the wildlife," it caught Jake and Lisa by surprise.

Then Jake said, "Yes, boys, they are so cute and cuddly, and to want to be wildlife conservationists when you grow up, we are so proud of you boys, but for now we must now all get ready to make our way back to the wildlife sanctuary. Lushand, and Abdul, can you help Ajay get the two cubs into the back of the jeep with Lady and watch over them, please, Mansou, Richard, and Vinh will be riding with you. Then followed by Max the vet in his van who is then heading off to visit a small village up in the mountain to check on a herd of Yaks, and goats with a few blue sheep (Bharal), that the villagers kept."

He then said, "Lisa, if we can get the boys into the other truck, with Jamie, Rachel, and Mike, while I go over and pay our respects to the village elders, the Buddhist monks, the villagers and the support teams?" then he paused and said, "You have to love the Nepalese people for their love for each and the love for their wildlife."

Once Jake had said his farewells, he then headed back to the truck As they left, the villagers, Gurkhas and all the support teams lined up and waved goodbye to them all, a very emotional and touching sight. (Playing on the radio was 'Love Is Here' by the Supremes). It truly lifted their hearts within the truck, then Lisa turned and looked into Jake's eyes, that spark had lighted up something special between them both.

Lisa on the way back turned to Jake, while the children who were now all fast asleep, then said, "Will the villagers be OK? What a tragedy, and it has been such a sad couple of days, full of emotion and turmoil."

She then said further, "It proves how fortunate and lucky we all are living in England, certainly an eye opener to experience by visiting such a beautiful country, the lush forests, the amazing wildlife, the wonderful people, but then to see how volatile the environment is here that can cause landslides destroying everything in its path, so terrible and heartrending to witness."

Jake then said, "Yes, it is so sad, but I have had experience of these natural tragedies and the problems they cause, as you say it is very upsetting, and it never gets any easier over time, but the villagers have the good support of the Nepalese disaster agency, from the other villages, and of course us all here, we will pop and see how they are doing, it is the least we can do to help. The Nepalese people have a special place in my heart, but that can be said with the many people from across the world that I have had the pleasure of meeting, but never forgetting those I met and lost during the last world war. It still catches me now and then" spoken with such emotion in his voice.

Lisa then said, "I know, my love. David would say only a few things to me about the last war, but kept most of what he experienced to himself. I wish he could have been more open, but my father said when he was serving in the First World War, it is hard for a soldier to open up to others. Sometimes I would hear him crying in his bedroom. It would break my heart. The times I did approach him all he could ever say, without looking at me, was that he had some dust in his eyes, making his eyes water," Lisa then said, "when we get back to England, I am going to make people aware of the fragile world we have had the pleasure visiting, and to help set up a fund to help the people in Nepal and other countries. The world needs to be made more aware of how fragile our world is, and also to do more to help the wildlife and the very precious habitats that these wonderful creatures share with this world," said with such compassion and love from the heart.

"That is a good idea, Lisa, the more affluent and wealthy parts of the world should contribute more to helping the less wealthy countries, and the wonderful wildlife, the amazing people, I am all for that," said Jake, in a jubilant and happy tone.

Finally, the team arrived back at the conservation centre (sanctuary) the children, so tired by now after a long day went straight to bed, while some of the team set up a secured makeshift nursery in a corner of the sitting room for Lady to look after her two snow leopard cubs and making sure they were fed for the night, before they all finally settled down for the night, except for Jake, as he was the first on the roster list to watch over Lady and the two snow leopard cubs, joined by Abdul, until he was finally relieved by Vinh and Mansou, who would take over in the morning.

Lady now started to settle down for the night, making sure the two cubs were warm, and snuggled up to her. Alex watched on, touched by Lady's natural motherly instinct to care for the cubs.

Over the rest of their stay in Nepal, the children learnt more, especially about the customs, the way of life, the animals and their amazing habitats from the Sherpas, local villagers, the conservation team, and of course from Jake.

The children were also invited a few times to the local Gurkha barracks to see what life was like as a soldier, and to visit the local school where Jake, with a couple of members of the conservation team were to talk about wildlife conservation. Jake's view was to get the children at a young age, to sow the seed of wildlife conservation, caring for the various habitats and the precious wildlife, animal husbandry. Sometimes Jake would be joined by Max the vet, who would talk to school children about being a vet and the important role the vet plays in wildlife conservation, and also looking after the various domestic pets.

David, Ben, and Omar, truly enjoyed their time, especially watching the two snow leopard cubs start to grow, overseen as always by Lady, a wonderful mother to them both.

The children also spent many happy hours playing ball with Lady and the conservation team. Lady had her moments, especially when she pierced the ball causing it to deflate, much to everyone's amusement and laughter.

The children also loved watching the various insects that lived around the buildings, including various colourful stick insects, grasshoppers, butterflies, and the odd praying mantis that would be on the ceiling of the living accommodation, waiting patiently for its next meal.

They also spent some time visiting the local villages, especially the village that suffered the terrible landslide, and visiting the sky burial site a couple of times, this indeed gave a lasting impression on the children about how precious life is, about learning to care for each other, the animals, and the wildlife habitats that need further protection for all to enjoy now and in the future and it was extremely emotional for all,.

As for the two snow leopard cubs, they had grown and now were in one of the large secured enclosures for their own safety, so that they could learn to be more independent, and to keep more of a distance from human contact, as for one day, they would have to be returned back into the wild.

Though the cubs were still young, they were learning fast to play fight with each other, but when carcasses of meat were put into their enclosure, the cubs would start to pounce on the meat, and then drag away with them, to their own individual areas to proceed in eating, such a wonderful sight to see.

The children, especially, were fascinated by them, and as for poor Lady, she did miss them very much, and would go up to the pen and try to be close to them, the cubs still had the instinct to go up to Lady and rub noses with her, a very touching sight, that would catch the conservation team, Lisa and Jake. A tear would be shed.

But this was not the end for Lady, as she would find happiness soon.

It was a few days before they all were about to leave the conservation centre, that Max the vet visited to do a check on the progress on the two snow leopard cubs.

Max also brought with him this time, his male jet-black German shepherd called Ramesh, he was a young and truly handsome dog, and yes, Lady took a shine to him.

Max knew over time that Lady needed a friend and thought that his newly acquired dog, would give Lady a bit of happiness, she had been devoted to caring for others and it was time she had some happiness.

It was then that we noticed, while Max was checking on the snow leopard cubs, that Lady would disappear with Ramesh into the forest, all we could hear was them playing together.

When they returned together, there was an air of love and romance in their walk, and the way their tails would sway.

Lisa then said to Jake, "Well, I think Lady has an admirer now, look at the spring in her step, I am so happy for her."

Jake then said, "Yes, Lady has a very handsome suitor, Ramesh, he is a very handsome lad, and I would not be surprised if Lady will in due course be a mother to her own family of puppies, one day. She would make a great mother. I do hope so, and time will tell," as usual he was excited at the thought of Lady maybe having a litter of puppies one day.

"Oh," said Lisa, paused and then said, "yes, of course, Lady has probably come into season, that would make sense, as it is this time of the year we would have to watch Lady, as when she was back at home in Yorkshire, she would attract a number of the local male dogs, picking up on her coming into season."

"Well, my beautiful Lady, you could yourself be a mother soon," said Lisa in a happy tone to her voice.

Jake then said, "I think we need to keep this to ourselves for now until we return back to Yorkshire. Exciting times for us. Yippee."

"Oh, Jake, I know you are as excited as I am, but please keep your voice down, the children might hear, it is still early days, but Jake I am so excited I could jump in the air with excitement at the thought of Lady becoming a mother," said Lisa, with a smile on her face, and with such joy in her stride.

Then Jake said, "Well, those are two bits of news we will have to tell your father, Mr and Mrs Brown and family, and of course our children," excitedly.

Lisa then walked back to hut holding Jake's hand, with Lady following from behind, wagging her tail from side to side, ears pricked up and with such a walk, and with Ramesh by her side.

Well, finally the day came for Lisa, David, Jake, Ben, Omar and Lady to leave the conservation centre, an emotional morning as they all said their farewell to Richard, Jamie, Mike, Rachel, Abdul, Mansou, Vinh, the Sherpas, Max with Ramesh, some of the Gurkhas', the villagers and some of the school children. To them this was one big family. The children and Lisa were by now in tears, Alex, as usual, trying to control his emotions as best he could.

All the family walked over for the last time to see the young snow leopard cubs, the children looked so sad, having to say goodbye to them.

David turned to his mum and said, "can we not take these back to England?" trying to wipe the tears from his face.

"Oh, David, the cubs are better off here, this is their home, just think we have all given them a chance, and when they are old enough they will be able to roam the mountain as they should, we also have had a wonderful time in Nepal, we must treasure these memories, and Richard and the team will keep us posted on the snow leopard cubs' progress. Now, dry your eyes my love," said Lisa.

Omar and Ben, cuddling their father, then said, "We have had such a wonderful time, can we not stay a bit longer?" also wiping the tears from their faces. You could see this was hurting the children and having to say goodbye.

"Now, Omar, and Ben, we have a surprise before we leave Asia, we will be visiting the wonderful city Bangkok in Thailand, but, sons, Lisa is right, we all have had a wonderful time, now all, on board the jeep," said Jake.

Finally, Jake turned to Richard and the team, the people around and said, "Now take care all of you and thank you all for your hard work, my friends, please keep us posted on the cubs progress. Boy I am going to miss you all, God bless," then wiping a tear from his face, trying not to let Lisa and the children see his emotions.

As they climbed on board the jeep, driven by one of the Sherpas, called Ajay, they all then started to wave goodbye to everyone as they started to leave the conservation centre. The children waving with tears rolling down their face.

Then Richard, the conservation team, Max the vet started to wave back, Ramesh sat sad faced, ears pinned back, then started to bay, in response, Lady in the back of the jeep bayed in reply, the eyes around her face wet from the tears that she shed for Ramesh.

The Gurkhas lined up and saluted to them, with the Sherpas, villagers, school children lined up along the drive, waiving to them, a number wiping the tears from their faces.

While trying to keep a brave face, Lisa then said, "Jake how long will take for us to get to Kathmandu airport, and then to Bangkok city?"

Jake then said, "Approximately one hour from here to the airport, and then a few hours in the air to Bangkok city airport, I have booked us into a local hotel for the night, and then tomorrow we can visit the temples and the city, then we need to get to the Bangkok city airport to fly back to England. So I suggest children you all try and settle down, it is going to be a long day ahead for us all," said Jake, "yes I can see you yarning Omar, now try and get some sleep, young man."

So the children did as they were told, and started to settle down with Lady next to them for comfort, soon the children were fast asleep.

After a long journey, they finally arrived at Kathmandu airport, they all then left the jeep with their luggage, and then said their goodbyes to Ajay.

The children especially, gave Ajay a big hug, and thanked him, he was very much like a big brother to them.

Jake and Lisa then said, "Thank you, Ajay, for everything, and for getting us to the airport on time,"

Then Jake said, "please write to us, and keep us posted on everything going on, including the village that was damaged by the landslide, as well as all the events at the conservation centre, the snow leopard cubs release etc."

Lisa then said, "It has been a truly memorable experience for us all, yourselves, the Nepalese people, and oh, the wonderful wildlife, thank you," and then proceeded to give him a kiss on the cheek.

As for Lady, she then sat down in front of him and then gave him her paw.

"Why thank you, Lady, I shall miss you and all the family," Ajay said, and then he said, "especially you, Lady, you are one special dog, I am going to miss you," trying to compose himself as best he could, without getting upset.

Then Ajay said, before leaving them, "now, we have some gifts for you all from us at the centre, there is also a very special box as well, so please handle it carefully. Please open when you get to the hotel, now here is the export licence for the box and its contents for customs clearance, signed by Max the Vet."

The children at that point looked rather puzzled as to what may be in the box, all they could see were some holes around the sides.

They all started to wave to Ajay and then headed off towards the airport with the two porters, who had put their luggage onto the trollies.

David then said, "Mum, what do you think is in the box? There are no sounds coming from the box" excitedly.

"Well, you are all going to have to wait until we get to our hotel in Bangkok, now, come on, children, we all need to check in, and then head off to the Bangkok departure lounge," Lisa said eagerly.

They moved through the busy airport, followed by the porters pushing the trollies, by now another porter was leading Lady with her green coat on, and another porter was carrying the large box, containing some very special animals, to the animal section of the aeroplane, awaiting on the main runway, the aeroplane ready for departure.

Finally, they all started to embark onto the aeroplane, greeted by the friendly cabin crew, they all then started to settle down in their designated seats, the cabin crew then proceeded to make sure all the passengers were safely fastened into their seat, ready for the aeroplane to take off.

The journey took a few hours, Lisa and the children decided to try and relax, while Jake went off to check on Lady to see that she was alright with one of the cabin crew in the cargo section.

Lady seated in her pen was so glad to see Jake, barking in excitement, and wagging her tail.

Alex then said, "Lady, now you be a good girl, we will see you soon," then proceeded to stoke her on the head, then he said, "Now you have a good sleep, my love."

The cabin crew member, called Tamarix, said, "She is a beautiful and very well-behaved dog, I will stay and watch over her for you," then he said, "I am a bit puzzled as to what is in the large box, all I could hear was some movement within."

"Thank you, Tamarix, I will head back to my seat now, see you both when we land at Bangkok airport," said Jake.

Lisa glad to see Jake return, then said quietly as not to wake the children up, "How is Lady, is she OK? I do worry when she is not with us, has she settled down?"

"Lisa, do not worry, she is in good hands, the cabin crew member who was with me, called Tamarix, is staying with her until we land in Bangkok airport," said Jake.

"That is so kind of him," said Lisa, try to relax and settle down.

Finally, after several hours in the air, the captain then announced over the speaker system, for all the passengers and cabin crew to remain in their seats, as we are now approaching Bangkok airport, soon to be landing.

Once the plane had landed the passengers then disembarked from the plane heading for the airport terminal once they had been checked by the airport security team, they all sat and waited for their luggage, the special box, and arrival of Lady.

Then all of a sudden, a bark could be heard, and Lady excitedly appeared, wagging her tail, led by Tamarix, followed by several porters carrying their luggage and the box.

The children in excitement raced over to greet Lady, hugging and kissing her.

Jake and Lisa walked over towards lady, and proceeded to make a big fuss over her.

Then they said, "Thank you so much Tamarix for looking after Lady for us, we are so appreciated."

Tamarix then said, "It was a pleasure, Lady is so well behaved, and I do love her green coat, she is a very special dog."

Then they all headed off to a nearby taxi, the porters then loaded the luggage and box into the back of the taxi, the children then sat in the back seats with Lisa and Lady, while Jake gave a tip to Tamarix and the porters, and thanked them.

Then the Taxi driver drove them off to their hotel, called The Golden Dragon, on the outskirts of Bangkok.

Well, the hotel certainly lived up to its name, a huge caving above the hotel doors of a golden dragon holding a pure white pearl.

The hotel staff greeted them with wreaths of white and yellow orchids, and then started to place them around each of their necks, while the porters placed the luggage and box onto the trollies to be wheeled into the hotel.

Jake stood outside with the family and Lady to have photos taken of them, then thanked the staff and then they proceeded to go inside the hotel, they were greeted by a water feature with a large golden dragon this time, holding the pure white pearl in its mouth, the children, especially, were taken back with awe.

Lisa said, "Now, children, let's wait for Jake while he registers us at the hotel, then we can go to our room and freshen up."

So the family then followed the two porters up the stairs to their room, number 33, they all then entered, the porters placed the luggage and box down by one of the tables, and then left.

Jake then let Lady off her lead, she then proceeded to go over to the box with some air holes around the sides, and gently she then pawed the box.

"Now, Lady, be patient we all are keen to see what is inside the box," he said as the family gathered around in excitement. Jake opened the box to reveal inside three seal point Siamese kittens looking up at them, Lady then gently sat looking at them in amazement and was mesmerised by them

The children then all said, "Please can we hold them?"

Lisa then said, "Right, boys, I will lift each one out of the box for each of you to hold gently."

The children then lined up ready to be given a kitten each to hold.

Omar then said, "What fat little bellies they have, what beautiful black brown markings, and with such wonderful blue eyes."

Lisa then said, "With such a long journey I would have thought they would be hungry by now."

Jake then said "I have a confession, Tamarix mentioned it to me when I said goodbye to him at the airport, it was then that he said, he was so keen to see what was inside the box, once he saw what they were, he then fed the kittens and Lady while on the plane, that is all I knew. To have three adorable Siamese kittens, what a wonderful gift for us to be given by all the staff at the conservation centre and the Nepalese people from the local villages."

Jake then said, "Now, children, I will check the sexes of the kittens," then said after a few minutes, "Well, we have two males and one female kitten, so please think of some names for them."

"But for now boys, please place the kittens back into the box so that they can lay on their little blanket, while I go down to reception and order some fish and water for them, and I suspect Lady you would like some food, your eyes say it all, "feed me". Oh you big softie, but we all love you," said Jake smiling.

"Now children, have you thought of some names for the kittens?" said Lisa.

David then said, "Can one of them be called Tao?"

Then Omar said, "One called Sasha."

And then Ben said, "Jaylin for the female as she has such beautiful blue eyes," he then started to giggle and then the other boys laughed, he then said, "like my blue eyes."

After a short while Jake returned, with a tray of food, Lady as usual was by the door to greet him as he came in, sensing, as usual, food on the way.

"Well, well, Lady, I see you are first in the queue for food," said Jake, as he walked over to the lounge and placed her food and bowl of water on the floor near the window. Lady heartily tucked into her meal, followed by a good refreshing drink of water.

Meanwhile, the kittens had their meal in the bathroom, after eating, they then drank some water. Lisa had put a toilet tray for them to use, then finally she proceeded to place the kittens back into the box for the night, where they duly snuggled up to each other and went to sleep.

"Well, children, have we got names for the kittens," said Lisa, see the excitement in their eyes.

The children all said, "Yes, the two males are to be called Tao, and Sasha, for the little female she is to be called Jaylin," in a happy tone.

"They are very nice names you have chosen, now we must all get ready as I have a surprise for you all. We must take Lady with us, as she will want to go around the nearby park to exercise, before we travel on to any great event," said Jake in an excited tone.

Lisa then said, "Right, let's make sure the kittens will be OK while we go out, now, come on let's see what the surprise is that Jake has promised us," pondering on what the surprise has installed for all of them.

The children eagerly jumping with joy, "Yippee," they all said in excitement, with Lady responding by wagging her tail from side to side, and titling her head from side to side.

"Now, all of you, keep the noise down, you will wake the little kittens up, I am as excited as you," said Lisa, and then she turned to Jake, and said, "You tease Jake, but I am as excited as the boys," then smiled at him.

They all then left the room, closing the door behind them, went down the stairs, and then left the hotel, heading towards the large park, full of scented shrubs, a grass area, and a large pond with colourful Koi carp swimming happily about.

Lady was allowed to be off her lead and to play with the children.

David then turned to Jake, "Please Jake, what is the surprise?"

"Well, David, you, Ben, Omar, and Lisa will have to wait and see," Jake said, with a big smile on his face.

After a while of playing with Lady, Jake then said, "Are we now ready?" they then headed off out of the park to where there was a massive group of people lined up, they all joined in with the group now waiting for the event.

Then, suddenly, a band of musicians appeared playing cheerful music followed by jugglers, and acrobats, then appeared a golden dragon with a large white ball in its mouth, followed by young men and women demonstrating the various types of martials arts movements for example the tiger, praying mantis, eagle and so on.

The crowds continuously gave rounds of applause and cheering at the entertainers, as for the children, you could see they loved every moment, joining in with the cheering and the clapping of hands. On a number of occasions the children's' jaws started to drop with awe, they were truly loving every moment, and totally amazed with it all.

Lisa then held Jakes hand tightly with Lady sitting next to her admiring the wonderful events, tilting her head from side to side, catching every sound being made, and wagging her tail from side to side with excitement.

Lisa then turned to Jake and said, "Thank you, I so do love you," and proceeded to kiss him on the cheek.

"There is more to come Lisa, just wait and see, you and the children will love what is to come," Jake said, in an excited tone to his voice.

Behind the crowds of people, by a nearby alley, was a hooded man robed in grey, watching on and smiling as the people were enjoying themselves with all of the entertainment. He then raised his hand to the sky above, spoke some ancient words, and with that the Shakra stone around his neck started to glow, and then the sky above started to light up, with various coloured fireworks, creating various colourful images of dragons, peacocks, butterflies, phoenix, tigers, flying horses, sea dragons, unicorns, eagles and many more animals being reviled, the colourful displays carrying on for some time.

Then he said, "such joy, happiness, but with such innocence."

While the crowds just loved what they were seeing, the children especially loved every moment, pointing on several occasions to Lisa and Jake at the various animals and mystical creatures in the sky above.

Then the man smiled again, and then clicked his fingers, the sky above then opened up, then he called for Maysu, a bright light then shone down on him and he disappeared out of sight, without the crowds even noticing.

The entertainment continued right into the evening, then Jake took Lisa, the children and Lady back into to the park, where a group of people were dancing to music on the radio, they then stopped to watch the dancers.

Then a special song was starting to be played on a radio, "Unchained Melody", Jake then turned to Lisa and said, "May I have this dance Lisa," with a soft and loving tone to his voice.

So they held each other closely as they danced to the music, tears rolled down Lisa's face, it was a song that she and David would dance to.

While the children started dancing with some of the Thai children, Lady was watching on, wagging her tail from side to side, and then a young woman approached Lady.

The young woman was robed in pale blue, with a metal band on her head with a symbol on the front of the band with the symbol of the moon, she then gently began to stroke Lady. Lady then gave her a paw, she then said, "Thank you, and bless you my friend."

Then she said, "Well, Lady, it is an honour at last to meet you. I must go now as your owners are approaching, we will meet again, my friend."

Finally, Jake, Lisa and the family with Lady, started to leave the park, heading back towards the hotel, the children by now tired out after the exciting evening.

Once they all arrived in their hotel room, Lisa got the now tired boys to bed, while Jake checked on the Siamese kittens, all fast asleep, Lady proceeded to lay by the bed where the children were sleeping.

Then Lisa went to the balcony where Jake was looking out towards the park, listening to the music which was being played on a radio nearby "If I Had Words," Lisa then embraced Jake, as they looked on at the park where people were still dancing, enjoying themselves, and them singing to the song, "Please Don't Go."

The following morning, after a hearty breakfast of cereal and fruit, after making sure that the kittens had been well fed, Jake and the family with Lady, left the hotel room, heading out of the hotel towards the park.

The children then started to play with Lady in the park, while Lisa and Jake sat on a bench watching the children playing with each other and Lady.

Lisa then turned to Jake, and said, "We have had such wonderful times, and I just cannot believe how the time has flown, this time tomorrow we all will be flying back to England," with a sad tone to her voice.

Jake then said, "Yes, it has been truly amazing, Lisa, time has flown so quick, we have had such wonderful adventures together. The children and Lady have truly loved every moment."

Then Jake and Lisa got up from the bench and then said, "Come on children, let's explore this wonderful city."

As they explored the various streets, markets, finally they came across a Buddhist temple.

Lisa then said, "I would like to go inside."

"OK, I will take the children to watch the magician nearby who is now drawing a large crowd of people, and then we will meet up with you at the Buddhist temple," said Jake, and then he said, "Come on, boys, and you, Lady, let's see what magic this magician is going to conjure up."

"Maybe the magician will turn you all in to fluffy white bunnies," Jake said, laughing.

Then Omar said, "Ha, Ha, that's very funny dad," then with that all the children started to giggle, Lady just sat and looked puzzled, but then she started to wag her tail, in excitement.

The magical tricks that the magician was conjuring up was awesome, from a white dove to appear from a hat to clicking his fingers thus causing fire flies to appear. He asked us to stand back while he then proceeded to light a very tall white candle on a stand, the flames creating images, from a fire breathing dragon, a phoenix, the face of a tiger, which then roared, to colourful butterflies etc. The amazing tricks kept coming, causing the crowds to applaud with joy, the faces on David, Ben, and Omar said it all, and again their jaws dropping.

Then, while Lisa was visiting the nearby Buddhist temple, admiring the wonderful statutes and the beautiful architecture within the temple, which was also being admired by the many visitors and Buddhist monks who were passing her by, all of a sudden she was approached by a hooded figure robed in grey.

He then stopped and said, "Lisa please do not be afraid, I will not harm you," in a gentle, friendly and reassuring tone to his voice.

Lisa then said, "Please, who are you, and how do you know my name?" in an inquisitive tone to her voice.

"Lisa, I understand that you may be shocked, but, please, hear what I have to say, it is so important and will play an important part in your life," he said caringly, and then gently holding her by her hand, trying to reassure her.

Lisa then said, "please, do continue, but may I know your name first?"

"Lisa, I understand, but my name must remain unknown to you for now, in due course all will be revealed to you, but what I can say is that I have your good intentions to heart", then producing from his robe two medallions on silver chains, and then he handed them to Lisa, by now looking totally surprised by it all.

He then said, "Please, for now, take care of them, they will play an important in your life, the world, and for two other people in the not-too-distant future, but for now, I will visit you again soon, and will tell you more then, please be patience my child."

Lisa, then carefully examined the two medallions, one side had the figure of St Christopher with Christ on his shoulder, and on the other side, a triangle with a dot in each corner, and a dot in the centre, then she looked at the man, and then said, "I do not understand what does this all mean and why me?"

Then she said further, "Is this a coincidence by chance as around my neck is a silver chain with a medallion that on the one side is an eagle clutching the sun in its claw, and the other side is the symbol of triangle with the dot in each corner, and one in the centre. I was given the medallion by my mother when I was a little girl, she said one day the medallion would play a very important part in my life, and to look after it carefully, as it is part of your heritage and where you came from, that was all she ever said to me."

"Well, Lisa, that has answered a question, why you were chosen by me, and secondly, as to your heritage, your ancestors came from an ancient world, steeped in mystery, magic, nature, caring and above all a compassionate race of people, a world protected by the guardians," he said with a smile on his face.

The man then said, "I understand, Lisa, this is a lot to take in, but please trust me, all will be revealed to you for now, take care and say nothing please to anyone, until I see you again back in your homeland in Yorkshire. I must go now, as I can see your son and friends looking for you, goodbye, my child, until we meet again, and all will be revealed."

Lisa then safely put the two medallions into her pocket, and then said goodbye to the man, "Until we meet again," in a puzzled and caring tone to her voice.

Then Lisa turned to see her son and friends approaching her from the distance, and then finally, she then turned back for the last time, but the figure robed in grey had vanished, nowhere to be seen, puzzled as to how can this be so, magic perhaps. (Music from Petit Papa Noel).

Finally Lisa was reunited with Jake, the children and Lady. The children started to tell her about the magician and all the magical trick he conjured up.

David then said, "It was truly spellbinding, Mum, I wish you were there with us," so excited at what he had seen.

Omar and Ben then said, "Oh, the magic, the fire breathing dragon, it was especially magical, right dad?"

Jake then said, "Yes, the magical tricks the magician conjured up were truly awesome," then he said, "Did you enjoy looking around this beautiful temple, Lisa?"

"The temple is so beautifully decorated, and a true homage to the Buddhist faith, I found being inside the temple was so tranquil, peaceful, uplifting, and just wonderful, Jake," said Lisa, still partly distracted by the visitor in the temple.

As they left the temple, passing the various streets, eventually arriving back at the park by the hotel.

Lisa then said, "Now, children, do you want to play for a short while with Lady? I just need to sit down for a few minutes."

Jake then said, "Are you alright Lisa? You seemed a little bit preoccupied in yourself."

"I am alright, Jake, just enjoying every moment while we are here It's just magical and the wonderful adventures we all have had together," then clasping him by the hand, "now shall we all go back to the hotel and see how the three kittens are?" said Lisa.

"So long as you are alright my love," said Jake, in a tenderly tone to his voice.

"Now come on, children, and you, Lady, back to the hotel now, we will have to start packing for our flight tomorrow morning, back to England" said Lisa.

The children then all said together, "Can we please stay out a bit longer" in an exciting tone, Lady barking and then wagged her tail.

"Now, children, we need to get up early to catch the aeroplane, so an early night," said Jake, then he said, "just think of all the wonderful memories you have had to treasure, and I have taken many photos of our travels together."

As they left the park, a nearby car radio was then playing 'One Night in Bangkok'.

Finally, arriving back in the hotel, and eventually arriving back in their room, they were greeted by the cries of the little kittens, they went over to see three little faces, with those adoring blue eyes, that would melt any heart.

Lady as usual went over to them giving them a kiss, and then proceeded to wash them, one by one, the kittens then started to purr lovingly.

David then said, "Isn't that so beautiful to watch? It reminds me of when Lady was caring for the baby snow leopard cubs."

"Yes, David, Lady is truly such a remarkable and affectionate mother," said Lisa, as she proceeded to stroke Lady on the head.

Then Omar and Ben said, "Oh, we have not opened the presents yet, which our kind friends in Nepal gave us all as leaving presents," excitedly.

"Right then everyone, I will go down and order the food for everyone, and will be back soon," said Jake.

"Come on then, boys, now, let's then open the presents together, and see what we have," said Lisa.

The presents for the children consisted of carved and hand painted animals and birds of Nepal, and a very well-illustrated book about the Nepalese wildlife, the people, and their customs.

Lisa was given a knitted shawl and hat, soft and warm, and a bottle of perfume with scented rose, lily and jasmine.

The children then said excitedly, "We wonder what present dad has been given."

Lisa then said, "We must wait for your father to come back to open his present, but look what Lady has, a colourful rope lead. Do you like it Lady? It is nice and strong". Lady turned and then barked, and then gave Lisa her paw.

"But, what is this children? The kittens have three pale blue collars with a medallion on them, when they are big enough for them to wear," said Lisa in a surprised tone to her voice.

"What wonderful presents we all have had, we must send a letter to thank them all," said Lisa.

Finally the door opened, with Jake and a porter carrying trays of food and drinks for everyone.

The trays were placed on the table, Jake then thanked the porter.

Then Lisa placed the bowl of food down on the floor for Lady to eat, which she ate heartily, followed by a bowl of water, which she lapped up and then went down to lay by the settee, falling fast asleep.

Then Lisa walked over to the box where the kittens were calling, "Well I see you are all hungry too," said Lisa, and then said, "now there, my little darlings, here is your bowl of food and water," which they all happily tucked into.

"Right, what goodies have we all got to eat and drink?," said Jake, then said, "well, there is macaroni cheese, with roast potatoes, followed by a sweet semolina pudding, also a variety of fresh fruit to choose from, and to drink fresh pineapple juice," and then he said, "now tuck in and enjoy."

They all then sat down around the table tucking into the food, and by now joined by Lady sitting next to David to see if any titbits would go her way.

"Oh Lady, you are so funny, tilting your head, and those soft brown eyes," said David. Then he, Omar, and Ben started to giggle at her.

"Lady you are so comical, you can only but laugh, I know you have given me your paw again, and looking with that sad little face, saying 'feed me' Now you have been fed, we will leave you something for later" said Lisa.

"Lisa, Lady will start to get fat with this rich food," said Jake, who then said, "I do not know where she is putting it, as she is nice and slim," said Jake, then he said, "OK well, oh, those soft brown eyes of yours would cause people's hearts to melt, you big softie," then stroking her on the head.

After they all had finished Omar then said, "Look, Dad, what we all have been given, but there is one present left unopened," he then proceeded to hand the present to his dad.

They all then looked excitedly as Jake then started to open his present. To his surprise it was a shirt with a design of a golden dragon holding a white pearl in its mouth, there was also a knitted colourful scarf with some of the Nepalese animals on it, Jake at that point was joked up with emotion welling up inside of him.

"What can you say? Such wonderful gifts, from such wonderful people," said Jake, brushing a tear from his eye.

The children by now were playing together with their new toys, while Lady was stretched out on a rug fast asleep and twitching, legs flicking, causing the boys to giggle at her, and by now the kittens were curled up together fast asleep in their box.

Jake then said in a puzzled tone to his voice, "Lisa, did you notice that the kitten's medallions have their names on them already, how can this be so?"

Lisa then turned to Jake and said, "Yes, you are absolutely right, the presents were unopened, so how could anyone know what we were going to call the kittens. I am as puzzled as you are, truly a mystery."

Well, that night while they children had gone to bed Lisa and Jake started to ensure that everything had been packed and ready to go with them tomorrow.

Then they both stood on the balcony looking out to the park, seeing people enjoying themselves, music was being played on a nearby radio, and the song 'I Can't Help Myself' (Sugar Pie Honey Bunch), and then the next song was 'Band of Gold', followed by 'Just One Look' sung by Doris Troy.

Jake then started to embrace Lisa, and then said, "That sweet perfume you have on, what is it my love?"

Lisa then said, "It is rose, lily, and jasmine, it is so fragrant, I just adore the beautiful exotic fragrance what a wonderful present to be given from our conservation friends and the people of Nepal," and then she embraced Jake tightly, whilst they both gazed out of the balcony as the sun was starting to set.

Next morning, they all got washed and dressed, then decided to take Lady for a long walk around the park with the children, who started to play with Lady and enjoying themselves, while Jake and Lisa sat cuddled up to each other on the park bench watching, and knowing soon that they will have to get ready to leave and fly back to England.

Then Lisa said, "Come on, boys and you, Lady, we need to head back to the hotel now," the expression on the boys said it all.

Then Jake said, "I know how you all feel, we all have had a great time in Nepal and Thailand, but maybe one day we will all return."

They all then returned to the hotel, went straight to their room and settled down to a light breakfast consisting of cereal, hot buttered toast, and refreshing fruit juice. Then Lisa and Jake moved all the luggage to one part of the room, ready for porters to collect.

Then all of a sudden came a knock on the door, one of the porter's then said, "Room service," then two porters entered the room, to collect the various luggage, the kittens had been put back into their secure cargo box, Lady on her lead with her green conservation coat on, sitting next to Lisa.

They all then left their room, following the two porters with their luggage heading down the corridor, then down the steps to the receptionist desk.

Jake then signed the register and thanked the receptionist and manager for a wonderful stay at the hotel, then he headed back to the family at the hotel entrance.

The family then left the hotel, while the two porters were loading the luggage into the taxi, Jake thanked them both and proceeded to give them a tip, as a thank you.

Once the family was inside the taxi, the driver then drove off to Bangkok airport arriving at around 7am, through the busy streets, where they were checked in, the luggage, and cargo box went off to the luggage bay, follow by Jake and Lady.

Jake then placed Lady into a secured pen with her cuddly brown teddy bear for company, and checked the cargo box with the kittens in to see if they were OK.

Then Jake stroked Lady, and said, "Now, Lady, be a good girl, cuddle up with your teddy," trying to reassure her, that they have a long journey back to England, then he said, "Now settle down and go to sleep, I will check on you later."

Lady then placed her paw in his hand, ears pricked back and the sad eyes, then he said, "Oh, Lady, I so do love you, I will see you soon."

The attendant in the luggage area, then said, "Please do not worry, I will watch over Lady for you," in a kind and reassuring tone.

"Thank you, I appreciate that," said Jake.

Then Jake headed back to the cabin, to find the three boys reading their books.

Lisa then said, "Are Lady and the kittens alright?" in a worrying tone.

"Lisa, Lady and the kittens are alright, the attendant is looking after them," said Jake.

Finally, the plane started to take off, the journey was long so the family after a having a mid-day meal, and Jake having checked over to see if Lady and the kittens were okay, decided to take a long nap.

Then over the loud speaker the captain then said, "Please can you all stay in your seats, as we are about to land at London airport."

The hostess then checked to see that all the passengers were in their seats, before they returned back to their seats.

Then the plane finally landed safely onto the runway and then proceeded towards the designated parking bay, before finally stopping.

Then passengers were all thanked by the cabin crew for choosing the airline, as they all started to leave the aeroplane, heading down the steps towards the main airport terminal and then finally heading off to the airline checkout desk, their luggage by now was moving towards the airport entrance ready for collection.

Well, as for Lady, she was being led by the aeroplane attendant in charge of looking after her, she was so eager to be reunited by her family, her tail wagging in excitement and carrying her teddy.

The attendant, called Paulo, then said "Now, Now, Lady, we are nearly at the airport entrance, and you soon will be reunited with your family, I am so going to miss you, my friend, and you are such a wonderful animal."

By now, Lisa had made a telephone call at the airport terminal lobby to Mr and Mrs Brown, to let them know that they will be arriving at Inkford train station around 10pm, with the sounds of excitement from Mrs Brown and David's brothers cheering in excitement in the background, with Layla and Troy barking.

Mr Brown then said, "I will be glad to have you all back home safely, I will meet you at the train station, with your father, until then, have a safe journey, pet."

Finally, they arrived at the entrance, where the family was, all excited to greet her, followed by two porters with their luggage, including a special crate with the three young Siamese kittens in it.

Jake kindly thanked the two porters for their help.

The children ran over to greet Lady, hugging and kissing her affectionately, as if they had not seen her for a long time, a very touching and emotional sight.

Lisa and Jake, then finally got their chance to make a fuss over Lady.

Then Lisa said to Paulo, "Thank you so much for looking after Lady, and the kittens."

Paulo then bent down to hug Lady, and whispered "Thank you, my friend, I will so miss you," then kissed her on the head.

Lady then responded by giving him a lick on the face and then her paw, Paulo was by now so emotional and trying to hold back the tears, the affects Lady had on him were so emotional it touched the family as well, then Paulo said, " Goodbye, my friend," wiping the tears from his face.

Lisa then said in a kind and gentle voice, "Thank you, Paulo, if you ever can come to Inkford village in Yorkshire ask for me at my father's forge, his name is Arthur Cook, or at Willow tree farm, the home of Mr and Mrs Brown. You will always be welcome to come and stay."

Then Lisa gave him a big hug and then kissed him on the cheek, which caused him to blush.

Jake then shook Paulo by the hand, and then said, "Thank you, my friend, until we meet again."

Meanwhile, the luggage and special crate was now inside the black London taxi, with the children now in the back with Lady, Lisa and Jake.

Paulo then said, "Thank you," and then he walked back inside the airport terminal, all choked up with emotion.

Then a man robed in grey stood next to Paulo inside the terminal, and then said, "Please, my friend, dry those eyes, do not be so sad, you will meet them again soon."

Then with that the man disappeared, then Paulo's spirits were all of a sudden uplifted, a sense of wellbeing came over him, as he then waved to the family as their taxi left, then he said to himself, "Yes I will meet them again," then smiled to himself as he headed back to the staff lounge to join the Thailand airways crew.

The taxi left the airport, heading in the direction of the London train station, ready for all to embark on their long journey back to Inkford train station, and then home to Willow tree farm for the night.

Finally arriving at the London train station, the two porters then came over to help them with their luggage, while Jake headed off to pay for the train tickets, then they all finally headed off towards the sign directing them to the northern train platform.

There they all sat down, awaiting patiently for the train that would take them through the beautiful countryside, onto the Yorkshire dales, and then reaching their final destination Inkford village railway station.

Then all of a sudden there came the sounds of the train whistle, and then the train appeared with white smoke bellowing from its funnel above, the train then came to a final halt at the platform.

Lisa and the family got up from the bench, waiting patiently for the passengers to leave their carriages, then they all approached one of the empty carriages, the porters then helped place their luggage into their compartment.

Jake then thanked the porters, then the children, Lisa with Lady and Jake entered the carriage compartment and sat down.

The children then settled down and fell asleep after their long journey, with Lady curled up fast asleep on the floor. Jake peered through one of the air holes to see that the kittens were asleep.

Lisa then said, "Well, Jake, not to long now before we arrive in Inkford," in an excitingly tone.

"Lisa, I shall not be sorry to relax at last, it has been a very long journey, but what a wonderful time we all have had in Nepal and Thailand. I shall never forget the wonderful people, the wildlife and the various habitats, what an adventure we all have had, and those wonderful memories we shall all treasure, and I will get the photos developed, taken from the camera as soon as possible," said Jake.

"Jake, it has been such a wonderful adventure, I cannot believe it has gone so quickly," said Lisa.

(Music from the film 'Out of Africa' playing on a nearby radio, as the train left London station).

Then they both settled down and fell asleep together, holding each other's hand, a sign of their affection for each other.

Finally after a few hours travelling through the various countryside scenes, the cities, towns, villages, the train stopping at various stations, finally the train came to a final halt, with the guard shouting Inkford station.

With that Lisa and Jake woke the children up, Lady half asleep, got up, and Jake kindly signalled for a porter to help him with their luggage and cargo box onto the railway platform. Then they all then left the train carriage.

Then Jake thanked the porter for his assistance.

Then, all of a sudden appeared around the corner was Mr Brown and Mr Cook.

Then they all fondly embraced each other affectionately, as it had been a very long time for them all and there was a lot of catching up. Lady, as usual was the centre of attention, those brown eyes that would melt anyone's heart and the wonderful tilting of her head, and the gesture of handing her paw said it all.

Then Mr Brown said, "It is great to see you all home again, you will have to tell us all of all your great adventures, though your wonderful letters gave us an insight to the special places you have all visited," and then he said, "as for you, Lady, you seem to have put on a bit of weight, my love," as he then stroked her affectionately.

"Yes, Lady has a bit, but that is another story we shall tell in due course, but for now let's all go home it's been a long day," said Lisa, now looking tired.

Then Mr Cook said, "Oh Lisa, by the way Lady MacCready came to see me the other day, and has asked to see you, once you have settled down from your overseas trip on a matter of mutual benefit". He then finally said, "I am puzzled as you are, Lisa, it sounds very interesting."

Lisa looked puzzled, and then said, "I wonder what it could be? Never mind, I will pop over to see Lady MacCready sometime tomorrow, if that is OK? Mr Brown if I could possibly use the horse and trap, please?"

"That is no problem, pet," said Mr Brown, then he said, "now let's climb on board the first horse and cart, followed by the second horse and cart with Mr Cook, Jake and the luggage."

On their travel they passed through the village, where they were greeted by various villagers, who they then started waving back at t, some of them shouted "Great to see you all, you must pop down to see us and tell us of your adventures in Asia."

Lisa then said, "We will pop down to visit you all soon, but thank you for such a warm welcome, and it is great to see you all again, take care," then started to wave back to them with the children, Lady sat up and barked at them whilst wagging her tail in excitement.

The villagers then said, "And great to see you too, Lady."

Finally, they all started to arrive back at the farm, where Mrs Brown, Oliver, Sam, Layla and Troy were all there at the farmhouse entrance waiting to greet them all.

First was Lady who jumped off the cart and ran straight over to greet Layla and Troy with the usual licks, sniffs, pawing each, with such affection.

Then the children climbed off the cart, and ran over to Mrs Brown, Oliver and Sam, clutching each other with such affection, the children excitedly mentioning about their wonderful times over in Asia.

Then Lisa climbed off the cart, with Jake from the other cart and approached the family with some of their luggage and the crate containing the Siamese kittens, while Mr Brown and Jake rode the horse and cart back towards the stables, ready to unharness the horse for the night back in his stable and Mr Cook tethered his horse to a post, ready to return back home later.

Then Mr Brown, Jake, and Mr Cook returned to farmhouse with the rest of the luggage, to be greeted by the rest of the family now sitting around the kitchen table drinking tea and eating a slice of fruit cake, while the dogs were stretched out on the large rug by the sitting room fire.

Then Mrs Brown said, "I have made you, Lisa and Jake a nice bed in the spare room, the children have the large bed that I have made up in David's room."

Then, all of a sudden, noises were started to be made within the crate, causing all three of the dogs to get up and start sniffing the crate with intrigue, Lady already knew what was inside the crate and then she started to bark at Lisa, trying to get her attention, while the other two dogs started to paw the crate.

With that the family started to gather around the crate, eager to know what is inside.

"Well Lady, you know, don't you my love," said Lisa, as Lady then started to paw the box gently, while Layla and Troy looked on and tilting their heads. Then she said, "oh, you funny lot, just look at you three," then smiled, while the three children started to giggle at the dogs.

Then Lisa, opened the crate top to the surprise of everyone in the room, three little Siamese kittens looked up and started crying, "oh my little darlings, just look at those soft blue eyes and those beautiful markings, they are just beautiful," said Mrs Brown, so stunned at the sight of their little faces.

Then David, Ben and Omar, started to pick up the kittens one by one and started to show the rest of the family, the kittens certainly loved the affection they were getting, starting to purr and rubbing their bodies against the family members.

Meanwhile, the dogs looked on wondering why they were not getting the affection of the family, then Jake said, "Oh, come over here, Lady, Layla and Troy, you big softies," and then they started to rub against Jake, Layla then rolled over to get her belly tickled, "you certainly love that, Layla," said Jake.

Then Mrs Brown said, "Oh, they are so gorgeous, but the little pets must be hungry," then she went off to the kitchen, followed in hot pursuit by the three dogs, then she said, "well whenever there is food about, the opening of the fridge door, you three are there Just look at those faces, those eyes saying 'feed me'. Well, my darlings, here is a dog biscuit each, now go and sit down while I get the food for the kittens, my loves," as she chuckled. Then she said, "Dad can you believe these three? Just look at them"

"I can mum, they are such characters, and attention seekers, but as I have always said you have to just love them, yes, especially you, Troy, your face says it all," said Mr Brown, with a smile on his face.

Then from the radio, a memorable song was being played, 'Hold Back the Night' sung by the Tramps followed by 'There Goes My First Love' sung by the Drifters. Mrs Brown started to hum to the songs and wiggling her body to the music, while preparing the food for the kittens.

Then finally, Mrs Brown came back from the kitchen, with a bowl of water, and a bowl of finely chopped up pieces of cooked chicken, then placing the bowls on the floor, then she said, "Let them eat in peace, while we all go back to the kitchen to have a mug of cocoa, freshly made sandwiches and homemade biscuits," and then she said, "and that goes for you three Layla, Troy and Lady, your bowls of food are now by the kitchen door."

"Hey, Troy, and that goes for you, now come on, you terror, your food is here, you daredevil, let the kittens eat in peace," said Mrs Brown, smiling.

Then off he trotted to join Layla and Lady to tuck into his bowl of food.

Then she said with tears rolling down her face, "I do miss them both so much, you can see their mother in them," then radio then started to play 'Love Never Dies'.

"Now, Now, my love, we all have fond memories of them both, they will stay in our hearts forever, I can see that Layla and Troy have inherited their mother's characteristics. Not a day has gone by that I have not cried for Lady and our son David," Mr Brown said as he then cuddled Mrs Brown, then he said, "now, chin up, pet, we have a new and extended family. What a joy, now let's settle down to together."

Then David said, "Nanny, please do not cry we all love you, I know in my heart Daddy and Lady are up there in heaven watching over us all," with a gentle smile.

Jake then said tenderly, "David, such beautiful and passionate words spoken by one so young," as he then proceeded to gently clutch Lisa by the hand with such tenderness, and love.

"Now, come on everyone, a toast to all those we have lost, but will never be forgotten and to those who are now part of our extended family," said Mr Cook raising his cup of cocoa, then looked at Lisa and David, and winked at them both.

Then the radio played the song, 'One Night in Bangkok', David then he said, "Mum, do you remember this song, that magic performed by the artists in Bangkok."

Then Omar and Ben said, "Oh, and the giant yellow dragon clutching a large white ball," as they said excitedly, and then giggled.

Jake smiled and then said, "Yes, Omar and Ben, the entertainment was pure magic, lifting your hearts and spirits. The music was just amazing, the smiles on the crowd's faces, watching and cheering as the entertainment progressed. The Thai people certainly know how to put on such a great show."

Then he said further, "Did you know that the white ball held by the yellow dragon represents a white pearl, and is said to bring good luck, happiness and a new beginning?"

Then Mr Brown said, "All sounds so amazing. Well, perhaps one day we must all go together on a holiday to Thailand, and Nepal, they certainly seem wonderful places to visit."

Lisa then said, "The people are just wonderful, the wildlife and the various habitats are just amazing, their customs and traditions, as Jake has said, the smiles on the people's faces touches your very soul, and yes one day we will all have a holiday in those fabulous countries, and you all can see for yourselves."

She then said, "The people just welcome you, many have very little in life, they are so proud of their race/heritage, customs and traditions, but more so their love for their wildlife and habitats is just so wonderful, we can learn a lot from them."

While the kittens tuck into their bowl of food, heartily, then drank some water from the bowl, they then finally started to lay down inside the basket with a warm blanket within that Lisa had made up for them, so content and cuddled up to each other for comfort.

At the kitchen table where everyone was tucking to a hearty meal made up of hot buttered crumpets, mugs of piping hot cups of tea, slices of fruit cake with a butter cream centre that had been baked earlier in the day by the Fortesque sisters, Penny and Betty, they all talked for an hour or so about their wonderful adventures to Nepal and Thailand.

Then Lisa said, "Now come on, children, it is well past your bedtime, say goodnight to everyone, and to the dogs and quietly to the kittens as they are fast asleep now."

David then said, "Oh must we Mum? We are all enjoying ourselves," with those gorgeous blue eyes inherited from his father, and that innocent look on his face, and then he said, "Please Mum."

"Now, David, it has been a long day for us all, up to bed now, tomorrow is another day," said Lisa. Then she proceeded to kiss him on the head, brushing back his brown curly hair.

Then Jake said, "Now come on, boys, that goes for you two as well, Omar and Ben" as he gave them a cuddle, then he said, "now say good night to everyone, and then off to bed."

Then the boys went over and kissed each member of the family goodnight.

"Lisa and I will be up shortly, boys, and I dare say, Lady will be joining you all," said Jake with a smile on his face.

Then Lisa said, "Oh, where are my manners?" as she went over to one of the suitcases in the sitting corner, and opened up one of them, to reveal inside a number of presents wrapped up, then Jake got up and helped Lisa carry the parcels back to the kitchen.

Then Lisa and Jake started to hand out the presents to the family, Mrs Brown had a bottle of jasmine, lily and rose perfume, Mr Brown and Mr Cook, each had a hand knitted scarf each depicting the with various wildlife animals on them, while Oliver and Sam each had a book on the wildlife in Nepal and in Thailand.

Then Lisa said, "And the other present is for Lady MacCready," then she said, "oh OK, Troy and Layla, you big softies, you both have not been forgotten, you both have a colourful rope lead each. Yes Lady I can see you tilting your head, just like yours," as she began to smile at the looks on the dogs faces.

Then they all then sat down for a few more minutes chattering to their heart's content. Then Jake and Lisa broke the news to them all that they have fallen in love and wish to marry. Silence in the air and then overwhelming joy, while Layla, Troy and Lady went into the sitting room to lay down on the large rug by the fire place, for a short while.

Then Mr Brown said, "We are so happy for you both, you can see the love you have for each other. Congratulations to you both, we will be more than happy to help you on this special occasion," by now Mrs Brown with tears of joy and the family then hugging each other, then he said, "a proud day for us all, and the children do they know?"

Lisa holding Jakes hand so tightly and then said, "They already know."

Then Mr Cook said, "Out of sadness comes joy and I am so happy for you both, your mother would be so proud if she was here, pet."

Then with that Lady, Layla and Troy got up from their long sleep on the rug, and proceeded to follow the children up to bed, "Well, I never they are on cue, as usual, you cannot but love the dogs, what a life they have," said Mr Brown, chuckling with laughter.

Then Mrs Brown then said, "Have you heard the wonderful news that has spread around the village of Inkford? Oh silly of me, you would not have known that Lady MacCready's head gamekeeper's female Labrador, called Honey, has been frequently visiting the nearby farm's, owned by an Australian sheep farmer, called Jack Foster, black Labrador, called Duke."

She then said further in an excitedly tone to her voice, "The outcome is Honey is soon to give birth, we all cannot wait to see the new puppies, the school children are all excited, they have been asking their parents if they can have one."

That reminds me, said Mr Brown, "Lady has certainly put on some weight, is she by chance going to have puppies?" smiling.

Lisa then said, excitedly, "Yes, we believe she is, we are all excited about her, and we know that she will be a fantastic mother."

Then Mr Brown said, "We better ask Mr Johnson the Vet to pop over this week to check Lady over then. On my way to Lady MacCready, tomorrow morning, I will call into to the surgery and make an appointment with Mr Johnson."

Then Mr Cook said, "Oh my, is that the time? I must make my way back home now," then saying good night to everyone, he then left by the kitchen door, then rode off heading back to his forge and house in Inkford village, waving as he left.

Lisa then turned and said, "Well, I think it is time for me to head off to bed, and check on the children."

Jake then said, "Yes, I am so exhausted, it has been a long day and bed seems a nice place now."

Lisa and Jake then said, their good night to the family, and then headed off upstairs.

While the rest of the family sat by the warm fire glowing in the sitting room, the three kittens all curled up fast asleep in their basket.

Then Mrs Brown got up and said, "Would any of you like a hot cup of cocoa before we all go to bed?" then she said, "well, Dad, it has been such an exciting and eventful day."

Then Mr Brown said, "Yes, it certainly has, and we all have an early start on the farm tomorrow boys, so a nice cup of cocoa will be a good idea, Mum," then he said, "we all can turn in for the night, tomorrow being another day for us all."

With that Mrs Brown headed off to the kitchen to make the cocoa for the four of them, then finally they all headed upstairs to bed.

Mrs Brown on the way up checked on the three children, she then turned to Mr Brown and said in a low voice as to not to wake up the children or the dogs, "Dad, isn't this just a picture, the children asleep with the dogs by their side."

"It is indeed a sight to treasure, my love," said Mr Brown.

The following morning, after breakfast, Lisa said her goodbyes to the family, as she headed off towards the farm yard, where the horse and cart was waiting, turning to the children and then said "Now, boys, all be good and I will see you later on."

Mr Brown then said, "Now, Lisa will you be OK to travel on your own, as you have had a long day yesterday."

"Mr Brown, I shall be OK, I'm in good hands, with Major," she then said, as she stroked his mane, then said, "I have missed you, Major," then turned and waved to the family by the farmhouse door.

Mrs Brown then said, "Give our love to Lady MacCready and to your father."

"I will, and give her and your father the basket full of homemade goodies I have prepared for them both," she said, with a smile on her face.

Then Lisa gave the command, "Walk on, Major," as they headed out of the farm yard, and then down the road towards the village beyond.

Mr Brown then turned and said, "Well, come on, lads, we have work to do on the farm."

Oliver, and Sam then said, "OK dad" with Sam still munching on a piece of toast.

Jake then said, "Come on, boys, it will a good experience to help on the farm as well. David will be able to show us the ropes," smiling.

"Well, lads, we have extra help, we soon will have the farm work done sooner," said Mr Brown.

Mrs Brown then said, "Now come on, take Lady, Layla and Troy in the back garden with you my darlings, and play for a while, while I feed these adorable kittens," she then turns to them, and said, "you are so adorable, those beautiful blue eyes staring at me. Oh you just melt my heart, and those beautiful marking on your bodies."

After a short, Lisa arrived at the forge, where her father was at work repairing a cart wheel, she climbed off the cart, and then said, "Now wait here, Major, while I see my dad. Major responded with a nod."

As she approached her dad, the radio in the forge was playing 'Cry for you' sung by September. The song certainly caught Lisa for a moment.

Then giving her father a hug then said, "A basket of goodies from Mrs Brown for you, Dad."

He then kissed her on the forehead, and said, "Aye, it's always great to see you, pet, and please thank Mrs Brown for the basket of goodies, which I shall enjoy very much."

"What a great night we all had. Are the children starting to settle down now after their wonderful time abroad?" he then said.

"Dad, it will take time for us all to adjust to the climate here after being in such warm and humid climates in Nepal and Thailand," Lisa said, and then said, "well Dad, I will pop over with the family during the week to see you, but for now I need to pop over to see Lady MacCready," giving him a big and a kiss on the cheek.

Lisa then said, "Love you Dad, see you soon," as she climbed onto the cart and then said, "walk on Major," and then waved goodbye to her dad.

After a while Lisa arrived at the manor house, where Lady MacCready and a nurse were helping a couple of wounded soldiers to their seats by the oak tree on the front lawn.

Lady MacCready spotting the sounds of the cart, then turned and said, "Hello, Lisa, I will be with you in a few minutes."

As Lisa climbed off the cart, she then turned and said, "Now, Major, be a good boy, I will be back shortly," and then proceeded to stroke his mane.

Then all of a sudden coming from the front door was a heavily pregnant young Honey, Lisa then knelt down to made a fuss of Honey, and said, "Oh, my love, it looks like it will be soon, and you will have some very adorable puppies, and what a great mother you will make."

Honey was enjoying the fuss being made, but then her attention was drawn elsewhere, nose sniffing the air, and then she started to sniff at the basket full of goodies next to Lisa, then Lisa said, "Oh, Honey, well you certainly love the smell of homemade cooked food, oh you are so adorable, those adorable eyes saying 'feed me'," then Lisa started chuckling to herself, and proceeded to stroke Honey on the head, and gently touching her velvety soft ears.

"Lisa, it is lovely to see you," said Lady MacCready, as she started to approach her from across the front lawn, then she turned and said, "and how are you Major?" he then gave her a nod, then bowing his head up and down.

Then she said affectionately, "Yes, it is great to see you Major, you handsome boy."

Then Lady MacCready, proceeded to give Lisa a motherly hug, then she said, "Now, shall we go to the drawing room?" she then turned and said, "Now come on, Honey, my love, you can lay on the rug, and rest, my love," as she petted her on the head.

They then finally sat down on the floral decorated chesterfield, while Honey laid down on the nearby rug and fell fast asleep.

Lisa then presented Lady MacCready with the basket full of homemade goodies from Mrs Brown, and her present from Lisa's trip to Nepal.

"Oh my, thank you, my love, and thank Mrs Brown, for such wonderful gifts and homemade goodies which I shall enjoy sharing with all at the manor, and the wonderful rose, lily and jasmine scented perfume, which I shall wear on special occasions," said an emotional Lady MacCready.

Lady MacCready then said, "Well, please tell me of your wonderful adventures to Nepal and Thailand". Lisa then started to talk for about half an hour of the wonderful experiences of the two countries, the adventures, the wonderful moments and the very sad moment at the sky burial, which caused Lady MacCready to brush a tear from her eyes, while enjoying the cup of tea and a slice of homemade Victoria sponge cake with strawberry jam and buttercream filling.

Lisa then said, "Now, how have you been? I see the hard work you are putting into helping the injured servicemen, it's just so wonderful and done with such dedication."

Lady MacCready then said, "I am well, but more so, it is a pleasure to help our wonderful boys, who dedicated their selves to serve their king and country. Such brave boys, but also never forgetting those that died" while never forgetting her family who died in the great wars, as she brushed a tear from her eyes.

After composing herself she then said, "Oh silly me, now Lisa what about you? I hear from your dad that you have fallen in love with Jake. What a wonderful match. I am so pleased for you both, if there is anything I can do to help on your wedding day."

"Why thank you Lady MacCready, I would be honoured to have you and if possible the medical and the servicemen at our wedding," said a joyful Lisa.

"Now Lisa, would you be happy if I have a marquee set up on the front lawn for your wedding day, with the local village band to play the music in the evening?" said Lady MacCready.

"I will ask Mrs Brown if she can help provide the food," said Lisa.

"I will also ask Cook, to liaise with Mrs Brown with the food and drinks preparations, as you will have a large number of people to feed, for it is a lot for one person to undertake, and I will ask James the gardener to provide the flowers for the church and the tables inside the marque," said Lady MacCready. Then she said, "We will make this a very special day for you both," then smiling at Lisa.

"Lady MacCready, you are so kind, and thank you," said Lisa.

"It is a pleasure my love, it is the least I can do," said Lady MacCready.

Then she said, "Now, on another note, as you know I have no immediate family. My husband and two sons died in the First World War servicing their king and country". Then she further said, "I know David had always loved working in the manor, as well as the gardens, and you, my love, have a strong passion for wildlife conservation; therefore I would like you, Jake and the three boys to come and live here with me. The house does need some life, and the injured servicemen will soon be returning back to their families and loved ones". By now Lady MacCready choked up with emotion, started to brush the tears from her eyes.

Lisa then proceeded to comfort Lady MacCready, as the tears rolled down her face. Lisa by now choked with emotion at the amazing offer, then she said, "We have certainly both lost some special people in our lives," as she brushed the tears from her face.

"Yes Lisa, I shall never forget them, there will always be a place in my heart for them until my dying day, when I will be reunited once again with them," said an emotional Lady Macready, by now Honey had woken up and sensed the sadness, started to brush her body against their legs.

"Oh, Honey, we must not forget you, my love, who will soon be giving birth to a litter of adorable puppies," said Lady MacCready, as she stroked Honey on the head.

Lisa then said, "I can only thank you from the bottom of my heart for all your kindness, and for your kind offer, Jake and the children will love to be here," as she proceeded to hug Lady MacCready affectionately, as a daughter would to her mother, and then whispered, "thank you."

Lady MacCready then said, "It would be a pleasure, my child, and the least I can do. Now, would you like to stay for some lunch with me, the medical staff and the servicemen in the great hall? I have already instructed my groom to feed and water Major at my stables."

"Why thank you, Lady MacCready, I would love to," said Lisa.

"Then that is settled, let us all head to the great hall. Yes, Honey, you too, after all you need to keep your strength up, my love," said Lady MacCready, patting Honey on the head, and then she said, "Come on my little darling". As they all headed off, Honey following wagging her tail side by side.

Well time passed by and it was now the day before Lisa's wedding. Preparations were being made for the wedding day. Mrs Brown busy in the kitchen baking various pastries, cakes etc., (while swinging her hips to the song on the radio, 'There Is No Stopping Us', sung by Ollie and Jerry) singing her heart out while doing the finishing touches to the wedding cake.

The children playing in the sitting room with the three Siamese kittens, Jaylin, Tao and Sasha, while Lady was stretched out by the fireplace on the large rug, next to her were Troy and Layla.

Sam and Oliver were helping their father with the farmyard duties, ensuring all the animals had been feed, and starting the milking of the cows in the dairy.

While Jake headed off that morning after breakfast to the railway station to collect their friends from Nepal, Richard, Jamie, Michael, Rachel, Max the vet, Vinh the Sherpa, Ajay and Mansou.

Lisa was then on her way to visit Lady MacCready, finally arriving at the manor house to be greeted by a joyful Lady MacCready, waiting at the front entrance of the manor house for her.

Then Lady MacCready said, "Oh, a joy to see you Lisa. Come, Come, I have a wonderful surprise for you," in an excited tone to her voice.

Lisa climbed down from the cart, and then turned to Major, "Now, you be a good boy," he then turned and nodding his head, she then proceeded to stoke him gently on his mane, and then she said, "I will see you later on."

A couple of soldiers then approached her and then said, "We will look after Major for you Lisa."

"Thank you both, and I hope to see you on my wedding day," said Lisa, excitedly with a spring in her step.

"We all would not miss your special day," said the lads.

Lisa then went over to Lady MacCready, and gave her a big hug, and then she said, "What is this exciting news, you have for me?"

"Come, Lisa, follow me to the drawing room, a wonderful surprise awaits you," said Lady MacCready, as Lisa follows her to the drawing room.

To Lisa's amazement, stretched out on the rug was Honey with six adorable puppies, suckling at her teats, with the head game keeper next to her, watching over them all.

Lisa then said, "Oh, what a wonderful sight, and aren't they just so adorable?" and then said, "When did Honey give birth to them?"

Lady MacCready, then said, "She gave birth to them in the early hours of this morning, she has just been a great mother, washing them one by one as she gave birth, and just look at the darlings, suckling at their mother's teats. What a joy to watch."

Lisa then said, "What a joy, two black and four cream/golden puppies. Oh, I could just cuddle them all, oh so adorable."

"Now, come on, Lisa, I need to show you the marquee," said Lady MacCready.

Meanwhile, Jake was seated at the railway station, waiting for the train with their friends.

Then suddenly from the distance was smoke billowing into the air. It was the train, finally arriving at the station and then coming to a halt at the platform.

Then suddenly, Mr Cook arrived at the railway station with his horse and cart, then he said to his tan female cob, "Now, Jess, we will wait here for Jake to appear with his guests and then we will head off to Lady MacCready's manor house," in a kind and gentle voice.

In the meantime, Jess was then starting to nuzzle up to Mr Brown's other shire horse called Caesar, a brown and white male, with the cart, that Jake had been using.

Then Jake watched eagerly as the train arriving at the station platform, slowly coming to a halt, with the final plumes of smoke wafting above. Then suddenly, the station master appeared with two porters to greet the people from the train.

Jake stood up from his seat, the carriage doors then started to open, as the people left their carriage apartments, heading towards the station exit, and carrying their belongs with them.

Then all of a sudden amongst the group of passengers, voices shouted, "There he is. Our Jake," in excited tones to their voices. Some wiping the tears of joy from their faces.

Jake then rushed over to them, greeting them with hugs, and then said, "I have missed you all so much," and then said, "come, my friends, our transport awaits you all, to take you to Lady MacCready's manor house, where she has kindly had rooms made for you all."

Then they all followed Jake to the two horses and carts awaiting them.

Jake then introduced them all to Lisa's father, Mr Cook. Then they all climbed onto the carts with their luggage, then, finally, they all started to head off towards the manor house, passing by some of the villagers, who started to wave to them, which they all then waved back to them.

Finally, arriving at last at the manor house entrance, all totally amazed at the size of the grounds, the large manor house at the front with stables and outbuildings to the side, and there awaiting to greet them was Lisa and Lady MacCready with a couple of her staff.

As the two horse and carts came to a halt, Lady MacCready said, "Welcome, welcome, my friends to our home," with a warm and welcoming smile on her face.

As they all then exchanged greetings, Lady MacCready then said, "Now, I expect you all need to freshen up after your long journey," she then turned to her two staff Hugh and Lucy, and said "please show our guests to their room and then we will all meet at the drawing room for a refreshing cup of tea, with an assortment of sandwiches and cakes to enjoy."

Jake then said to the guests, "I will follow you upstairs and then when you all are refreshed show you all back down to the drawing room."

Meanwhile, back at the farm, Mr Brown arrived inside the farmhouse kitchen to be greeted by Mrs Brown, by now boxing up the various food to be delivered to the manor house.

Mr Brown then said, "How are the boys settling down on this busy day?"

Mrs Brown said, "They are all enjoying themselves in the sitting room with the Siamese kittens playing with their soft toys. The dogs are fast asleep," and then said, "My only concern is that we have had moments with Lady becoming restless at times," in a concerning tone to her voice.

Mr Brown then said, "Well, Mum, I think Lady is nearing her time, we will need to gently get her onto the other horse and cart this afternoon, I hope she will be okay with the three kittens," in a sad tone to his voice. Then he said, "I am going to miss them so much, including Lisa, David, Jake, Omar, and Ben. It will not be the same without them."

"I agree Dad, it will not be the same, but they have a new life together, and it is not as if they will be a fair distance for us to see them. They are only up the road at the manor house, my love," said Mrs Brown, in a loving tone, and then kissed him on the cheek.

With that Sam and Oliver arrived in the kitchen, and they then said, "Mum, what is for lunch? We are starving."

"Well, my boys, come on everyone, I am about ready to serve lunch, macaroni cheese with mashed potatoes, followed by sultana sponge with custard," said Mrs Brown.

With that everyone rushed to the kitchen table to sit down and ready to tuck into their food. As always, they were followed by Layla, Troy and poor Lady waddling as best she could.

Mrs Brown then said, "Well, tuck in, and as always we have some uninvited guests to the table. Oh you three, those eyes say it all. Come on then, here are your bowls of food with some macaroni cheese as a special treat," then she said, "oh Lady you have a bit extra as you are feeding your unborn puppies," stroking her on the head, then said, "oh my poor darling, it will soon be over and you will also have a new family to look after, my love, you are so much like the old Lady."

After lunch Mr Brown guided Lady to the horse and cart, and then managed to get Lady to carefully walk up the plank of wood that leant against the back of the cart. Then Lady started to lay down on a large blanket, while Sam and Oliver handed their father the secured box containing the three Siamese kittens.

Mr Brown then said, "Thanks, Sam and Oliver," as he climbed onto the cart, then turning to the rest of the family with Layla and Troy by their sides waiting by the kitchen door, he said, "I will see you all later on. Sam and Oliver can you make sure that you check that all the farm animals are OK? And then we will bed them down for the night when I return," he then waved, as he then headed off towards down the farm tracks towards the village and then onto the manor house. Lady by now was fast asleep at the back of the cart.

Meanwhile, Lisa had now said her farewells to everyone at the manor and was now leaving with her father on his horse and cart heading towards his forge. As they approached, Lisa turned to her father and said, "Would you mind if I use the horse and cart to travel to the lane nearby the farmhouse and spend a couple of minutes by the stream, where they found David and Lady?"

"You go ahead, my love, and I will see you soon," said her father, then gave her a kiss on the forehead.

Lisa then headed off leaving the village behind her, and then headed off towards the stream, she then climbed off the cart, and said, "Now, Jess, I will only be a few minutes," then stroking Jess on the head, and then headed off towards the stream.

After Lisa said a few words by the tree next to the stream, where David would take her with Lady.

Perched at the top of the tree were two white doves, cooing to each other.

The memories then came flooding back, tears started to roll down her face. Then, all of a sudden, she turned to see a man walking towards her robed in grey.

He then stopped and said, "Be not afraid, my child, I mean you no harm. Well, we meet again as promised from our last visit in the Buddhist temple in Bangkok some months ago."

He paused and then said, "Have you kept the two medallions I gave you and have you said nothing to anyone of our last meeting?" in a gentle tone to his voice.

Lisa, then wiped her eyes, and then said, "Yes, I have kept my promise. No one knows of our meeting, and the two medallions are kept safe in my dressing room table. But why the secrecy?"

"Lisa, as I told you, one day those medallions will serve a greater purpose for two very special people. Until then, be patient, I will visit you again soon," he then said.

"Now, I believe you are getting married tomorrow morning, I wish you and your future husband, Jake, all the happiness in the world, but for now I will meet with you again soon," he said, and then turned to walk away.

Lisa then said, "May I know you name?"

He turned and then said in a gentle tone, "The people call me Symeon," smiling at her in a reassuring way, and then he disappeared out of sight, with the sudden sounds of beating wings.

Lisa then turned back towards the tree, to see above her, two white doves still cooing, the tears started to roll down her face, then she said, "I do miss you both so much, but now life has given me a second chance for happiness. But, my loves, I will always have that special place in my heart for both of you," wiping the tears from her face.

Then on the ground she noticed a metal bangle with ancient symbols inscribed on it, with a yellow dragon holding a white pearl brooch. Next to them was a bouquet of cream scented roses, sprays of pale pink jasmine flowers, lilies of the valley, with a spray of pale green cymbidium orchid flowers that gave of a very sweet fruity perfume. She then picked up the bangle, brooch and bouquet of flowers, and started to head back to the horse and cart nearby.

As she then turned back for the last time, a voice then said, "I hope you like the wedding gifts and flowers, until we meet again Lisa," then the voice faded into the distance.

Lisa then climbed onto the cart, gently placing the bouquet of flowers next to her, and the bangle and brooch safely in her coat pocket, then she said, "Jess, my love, walk on."

That night everyone was making the final preparations for the big day tomorrow.

On the early morning of Lisa's wedding day, Lisa decided to leave the forge, and started to head off to the graveyard to pay her respects to her soul partner David and their faithful dog, Lady, where they were buried together, to lay some flowers, next to the headstone.

Lisa then said a few words of respect, then all of a sudden she was approached by a beautiful young lady dressed in a long flowing pale blue dress, her long black flowing hair, and her pale skin with intense pale blue eyes, wearing a necklace with a symbol of the moon on it.

The lady stopped and said, "What a beautiful headstone, the inscription is very touching to two such wonderful beings. A remarkable tribute to an everlasting friendship between David and his devoted dog called Lady, they will always be watching over you, Lisa," with such kind and humbling tone to her voice expression on her face gave radiance and a peace of mind to Lisa, and then she said, "I hope you have a lovely day, on your special day, Lisa."

Lisa then said, "Thank you," but to her amazement the young lady had suddenly disappeared into a mist beyond.

Lisa looking somewhat puzzled, pulled herself together and then headed back to the forge, to prepare herself for her wedding day.

Upon arriving at the forge, her father was putting the finishing touches to the cart, finely decorated with flowers and ribbons, Jess had already been groomed and was now attached to the cart.

Mr Cook seeing Lisa approaching the forge, then said, "Come, my love, it is time to get ready, the wedding is about to start in an hour's time, Lisa."

"I will Dad," as she then headed upstairs to get dressed, in a long flowing dress of pale cream with soft pale-yellow trimmings, she then brushed her long flowing hair back, into a pony tail, then proceeded to dab the perfume from the Nepalese people.

Finally with minutes to spare, Lisa then proceeded to walk down the stairs, to be greeted by her father.

Brushing a tear from his eye, Mr Cook then said, "Lisa you are so beautiful, just looking at you, you remind me so much of your wonderful mother, God rest her soul, she, like me, would be so proud of you". He paused and then said, "Your carriage awaits you, and here is your bouquet of flowers, now off we go your groom awaits you, my pet."

Mr Cook then helped Lisa onto the cart, and then they headed off towards the church to be greeted by a row of soldiers, including a detachment of Gurkhas, lining up either side of the path leading up to the church entrance.

Lisa then was helped off the cart by her father, and then proceeded to walk up the church path, passing, along the way, the soldiers finely dressed in their uniforms, representing David's regiment, the Yorkshire regiment. It did catch her a bit, one soldier smiled and then winked at her, causing her to slightly blush, finally as they arrived at the church entrance they were greeted by her maids of honour dressed in long flowing pale green dresses, their hair tied back with a white orange blossom flower nestled at the side of their hair.

The door to the church was then opened, and Lisa with her father by her side, followed by the maids of honour, proceeded down the church aisle to the music played on the old pipe organ.

Finally, the wedding procession came to a halt at the altar. There she was greeted by the Catholic Bishop Jacob

O'Malley, with Jake and his best man to one side. Watching on were two Buddhist monks, who smiled at them both.

Jake turned to Lisa, and said in a soft voice, "You are so beautiful."

With that the wedding proceeded, with the exchange of wedding rings and vowels, then during the wedding various songs were sung by the church choir made up of adults and children from the local school, including 'All Things Bright and Beautiful', 'If I Had Words', and 'I Won't Leave You' (from Pompeii).

Then, finally after signing the register, Lisa and Jake, holding each other's hand, proceeded to walk up the aisle towards the church entrance door, followed by the maid of honour, then family and friends. The church door opened to be greeted by the soldiers lined up either side of the church path.

Meanwhile at the back of the church, by David and Lady's grave, stood the man hooded and robed in grey called Symeon, by his side was the young lady dressed in pale blue waiting eagerly to see the newly wedded couple, Lisa and Jake leaving the church entrance.

Symeon then turned to the young lady, and then said, "Well Kira, we will watch over the events as they unfold, for this will be crucial for Lisa, as she has a big part to play. But for now, I wish the happy couple all the very best and a very happy life together, we will meet Lisa again soon," with that he raised his hand to the sky, and a large colourful rainbow then appeared over the church. Sitting on an old apple tree nearby were two white doves looking down and cooing to each other.

Kira then looked up above to see the wonderful rainbow and then said, "Truly beautiful, my lord, Lisa has such a very crucial part to play and we need to watch over her, and to protect her from any harm."

"Have no fear, my child, she is safe, apart from us who will watch over her, in the wedding party are four special people who will protect her and you that I promise. Now I will have to leave you, Kira, and will see you again soon," said Symeon in a gentle tone, then with that he disappeared into a mist.

Meanwhile after a few photos were taken at the church entrance of the pair together and then family and friends, they then headed down the church pathway to be greeted by rows of finely dressed horses and carts. But for Lisa and David, a special carriage had been prepared for them by Lady MacCready's staff, they also had a small detachment of the Yorkshire Dragoons on their fine brown horses, arranged by Lady MacCready. They both were then helped into the open carriage, then their escort proceeded down the village heading towards the manor, followed by the family, friends on the various horse and carts, following behind them in an orderly fashion.

Meanwhile at the manor, Hugh, Lady MacCready's butler hearing the sound coming from the drawing room was greeted by a wonderful sight, he then said, "Oh Lady, what wonderful and adorable puppies you have just given birth to, what a wonderful surprise for everyone from the wedding party, then brushing a tear from his eye and choked with emotion. Watching nearby was Honey with her new-born puppies, nestled up close to their mother.

Peering through the clouds, watching on and careful not to be seen, he then said, "So this is what has been drawing Symeon's attention, well, for now may the newlyweds have a wonderful day, but I shall be watching on as the events unfold in the next story," then chuckling to himself.

Then all of a sudden the crystal pendant on a solid chain around Symeon's neck started to glow, a sense of warning, then he said to himself, "So he has arrived in Yorkshire. Well watch, my friend, watch, Lisa is well protected, and no harm will come to her, that I promise, her path, her fate and her future lies in my hands now."

As the carriage with Lisa and Jake with their escort finally arrived at the manor, behind them were the families and friends, in the horses and carts, then followed close behind by the rest of the villagers, and soldiers from the Yorkshire regiment and the Gurkha regiment?

The band started to play a selection of music as followed: 'Unchained Melody', 'Band Of Gold', 'Electro Velvet', 'We Meet Again', 'Land Of Hope And Glory', '(Your Love Keeps Lifting Me) Higher and Higher', 'If I Have Words' and so the upbeat songs go on right into the night, with people joining in, singing to their heart's content on this joyous occasion. The guests dancing to the wonderful music and also entertained by the Thailand and Vietnamese dance troupes, then amazing magical tricks performed by a special magician from Bangkok, but who is he.

From a nearby tree watched on, was two grey hooded robed men called Andreas and Karolus, smiling at the people enjoying themselves?

Then Andreas said, "Well our Lord Basu was right," in a soft tone to his voice.

"Yes my friend, the events are starting to unfold, nicely," said Karolus, with a gentle smile.

Lisa, Jake and the family with Lady MacCready left their transport and then started waving to the various friends, injured servicemen, medical staff, and so on. As they then headed off to the drawing room, the surprise on their faces was evident as they were greeted by Lady and her new puppies, watched on by Hugh, brushing the tears from his face.

Lady MacCready then said, "Oh, Hugh," brushing the last of the tears from his face, and with a reassuring smile from her face.

"It has been such a wonderful day, and to see Lady with her new born puppies, they are so adorable," said Hugh trying his best to compose himself, with Millie his spaniel by his side.

"Hugh you remind me so much of my sons," said Lady Macready in a gentle tone.

Then Lisa, by now choked up with emotions, and brushing the tears from her face, composed herself and then said, "Oh Lady, what a wonderful surprise, such a beautiful litter of puppies, you truly are going to make a great mother," then paused and said, "Honey we're not forgetting you, my love, what adorable litter of puppies, thank you."

The children looked in awe and with such excitement in their eyes, Jake clasping Lisa's hand, Mr and Mrs Brown and Mr Cook watching on trying to control their emotions.

Behind then watching on was Kira, the two Buddhist monks, Abdul and Vinh. Kira then said softly, "My friends, we must now watch over this young family, especially Lisa, as is our task, it is so vital to what lies ahead, as is the part we must play, crucial in the times now and to come, my friends."

With that one of Lady's puppies started to move his head slightly, pointing up in the direction of Lisa and the family.

Vinh then said in a soft tone to his voice, "So this is to be the young Ollie (black and brown puppy), I see we will need to watch over you young man and your mother Lady, an important role you must all play as the next story unfolds," with a gentle smile on his face.

"But for now let the puppies enjoy their time together with their mother, as for Ollie his future will become clear in time, and we must be ready to help him, Vinh and Abdul", said Kira.

"Then let us all enjoy this very special day, and wait patiently as the next adventure of Lady unfolds", said Abdul, in a reassuring tone to his voice.

"Then a toast my friends, here is to Lisa and Jake, long life and happiness", said Vinh, as they raised their glasses to the happy couple.

**Pip
and Hyperion**

Honey the Labrador